She gasped as she looked at the mess in her kitchen.

Someone had been in here, searching for...what?

Grabbing her purse, she looked for Jonathan Littledeer's business card. She found it and dialed the number.

"Littledeer."

"Detective, this is Lilly Burkstrom. I just walked into my house. It looks like my ex-husband's apartment wasn't the only place ransacked."

"Your house was broken into?"

"Yes."

A crash from the bedroom made her gasp.

"Lilly?"

"I heard something crash."

"Get out. Go next door and call nine-one-one."

She turned and ran out the garage.

Books by Leann Harris

Love Inspired Suspense

Hidden Deception
Guarded Secrets

LEANN HARRIS

When Leann Harris was first introduced to her husband in college she knew she would never date the man. He was a graduate student getting a PhD in physics, and Leann had purposely taken a second year of biology in high school to avoid taking physics. So much for first impressions. They have been married thirty-eight years and still approach life from very different angles.

After graduating from the University of Texas at Austin, Leann taught math and science to deaf high school students for a couple of years until the birth of her first child. When her youngest child started school, Leann decided to fulfill a lifelong dream and began writing.

Leann presently lives in Dallas, Texas, with her husband. She is a founding member and former president of the Dallas Area Romance Writers. *Guarded Secrets* is her second novel for Steeple Hill Books. Visit her Web site, www.leannharris.com.

GUARDED SECRETS
Leann Harris

Steeple
Hill®

Published by Steeple Hill Books™

STEEPLE HILL BOOKS

Steeple Hill®

Recycling programs for this product may not exist in your area.

ISBN-13: 978-0-373-44358-1

GUARDED SECRETS

www.SteepleHill.com

Printed in U.S.A.

God is our refuge and strength,
an ever-present help in trouble.
—*Psalms* 46:1

Jennifer, DQ, Daniel and Crystal—
each of you is a blessing.

ONE

The door stood ajar, and panic raced through her veins. She'd locked her ex-husband's apartment door after retrieving his clothes for the funeral.

"Mom, did you forget to lock the door? You know Daddy always made me—" Tears clogged Penny's throat.

Lilly Burkstrom pulled her daughter into her arms.

"I don't understand, Mom," Penny sobbed into her mother's waist. "Why did Daddy have to die?"

It was a question Lilly asked herself. Peter had been murdered in a convenience store robbery gone bad.

It didn't make much sense to her, a twenty-nine-year-old woman, so how could she expect her eight-year-old daughter to understand it?

"I don't know, sweetie. I know you miss him. I do, too."

Penny hugged her with a desperate intensity. "You won't leave me, will you?" She looked up, her huge brown eyes glistening with tears.

Lilly's heart broke. She wiped the wetness from

her daughter's cheeks. "No, I won't." Although she and Peter had been divorced almost since Penny's birth, they had come to terms with their failed marriage and had become friends. Peter's recent salvation had changed all their lives. "I can take you home and do this by myself."

Penny wiped away her tears and stepped back. "I want to help."

Lilly pushed the door all the way open and peered inside. The condition of the apartment shocked her.

Penny gasped. "Mom, what happened?"

Lilly's gaze swept the living room, dining room and kitchen. It looked as if a tornado had ripped through the place, throwing things everywhere. Chairs and end tables had been tossed on their sides. The sofa had been turned over, and the cushions ripped and thrown around the room. The kitchen cabinets stood open; boxes of cereal and spaghetti spilled out from the shelves. Broken dishes and glasses littered the countertops and floor.

"I don't know." Three days ago, when she'd been inside this apartment to get one of Peter's suits for the funeral, everything had been fine.

"I wonder if Dad's bedroom is this way." Penny started down the short hall.

A loud noise came from the bedroom.

Penny froze. When she turned her head, her frightened gaze met Lilly's.

Lilly motioned for her daughter to come toward her. Penny turned and ran to her mother. Lilly rushed them out of the apartment and down the stairs. They retreated to Lilly's car, and Lilly whipped out her cell phone.

"Nine-one-one. What is your emergency?"

"I need to report a burglary."

Detective Jonathan Littledeer greeted Lilly outside Peter's apartment door.

"Ms. Burkstrom, can you tell me what happened here?"

She recognized the Albuquerque police detective and his partner, David Sandoval. They'd come and told her about 'Peter's death. Had it only been two weeks since that happened? It seemed like it was yesterday when they announced the grim news.

Stepping inside the apartment, Detective Littledeer stopped and scanned the area between the front door and the living room.

"Someone did a job on this place," Detective Sandoval murmured, walking around the living room.

Detective Littledeer looked around the living room and kitchen. "It looks like they did a thorough search. What do you think they were looking for?"

Detective Sandoval nodded. "Good question. I'll take a look in the bedroom." He disappeared into the bedroom.

"Where's your daughter?" Detective Littledeer asked Lilly, who was standing in the doorway.

"She left with my cousin. She didn't need to be here. It upset her." Lilly had called her cousin Allison and asked her to come and pick Penny up. Allison was one of the few family members left in town after her parents moved to Florida. Alison had a child younger than Penny. They'd been friends all their lives, and Penny needed a friend to help her redirect her thoughts.

Spying a digital picture frame on the floor, Lilly picked it up. "Peter bought this for Penny so she could see pictures of the two of them having fun." She placed the frame on the coffee table.

"Can you think of why anyone would do this to your ex-husband's apartment?"

"A couple of months ago, when Peter dropped off Penny, he told me that if anything happened to him, it wouldn't be an accident."

"Did he tell you what he meant by that?" Detective Littledeer asked, pressing her.

"Later, when I tried to question him about it, he simply shook his head, kissed my forehead and asked me to pray for him." She looked down at the floor. "I tried to get him to explain a couple of times after that, asking him exactly what he meant, but he wouldn't tell me anything. He acted like I had imagined it."

"The bedroom's in the same shape as the rest of the place," Detective Sandoval informed them as he joined them in the living room.

"Was someone in there?" Lilly asked.

Detective Sandoval glanced at Detective Littledeer before turning to her. "Yeah."

She stumbled to the sofa. "Penny almost went in that room."

Detective Littledeer squatted in front of Lilly. "But you didn't let her, did you?"

"No. I didn't," she replied.

He covered her hand with his. When she looked at him, he smiled. "A mother's wisdom is from above." He stood. "Ms. Burkstrom might have an angle on this," Detective Littledeer told his partner.

"What's that?" Detective Sandoval asked.

"Her ex had been threatened."

Detective Littledeer motioned Lilly toward the kitchen table as the crime-scene people arrived and started taking prints. "Is there anything you can think of that your ex-husband was involved with that was risky?"

Lilly tried to come up with something suspect that Peter could've been involved with. "I really don't know of anything. After we divorced, he started drinking and running around. He'd show up sporadically at the house and want to see Penny, and then he would disappear again for six months.

"About four years ago, he found a job and seemed to straighten up his life. He saw Penny regularly and paid his child support. Eighteen months ago, he started coming to church again and gave his life to Christ. He seemed very happy until—"

"Until when?" Detective Littledeer quizzed.

"It was last April. I remember when because it was right after tax time. He'd glanced at my tax return and got a funny look on his face. He turned to me and gave me that warning."

Detective Sandoval walked into the kitchen and sat down next to Detective Littledeer. "The evidence team's finding lots of prints."

"How will you know if they are Pete's or someone else's?" asked Lilly.

The detectives looked at each other. Detective Littledeer met her eyes. "Your husband's prints are on file."

She paled.

"It was a drunk driving charge from four years ago," he explained.

Lilly wondered if they were telling her everything. "Is that all?"

"Also, the company he was working for at the time of his death requires prints of all its employees," Detective Sandoval added.

Frowning, Lilly asked, "Why would they do that?"

"Armored car personnel have to have their prints on file," Detective Littledeer explained.

"We'll also need your fingerprints," Detective Sandoval added.

Her heart raced. "Why?"

Detective Littledeer frowned at his partner, but he turned to her. "Simply as a process of elimination. Also, bring your daughter with you so she can be fingerprinted. You can tell her that it is just a precaution. Schools now like to have the kids fingerprinted."

He didn't say why, but Lilly knew the sad reality of missing children. One of the women who worked with her at the church and the community garden had a child who'd gone missing.

"I'll bring Penny by tomorrow and we both can have our prints taken."

"What's going on here?"

They looked up and saw a man standing in the doorway. In his early fifties, he stood with a military preciseness and his hair was cut in a burr.

"And you are?" Detective Littledeer asked.

"Mark Rodgers, the owner and manager of these apartments." He glanced around the room. "What happened here?"

After informing the owner who they were and why they were there, Detective Littledeer asked, "Did anyone ask to see this apartment in recent days?"

"No. No one has been by to ask anything. Since Mr. Burkstrom's lease was up at the end of the month, I wanted this place cleaned out so I could paint and recarpet. He bought a new condo off of Rio Grande Boulevard."

"When was the last time you were in this apartment?" Detective Sandoval asked.

"I came by when this lady here got her husband's clothes. I told her then when the lease was up." The owner looked around at the mess. "This place wasn't this way the last time I was here."

"Did you see someone leave here in the last half hour?" Detective Littledeer asked.

"No. I just got back from a trip into Santa Fe. When I saw all the cop cars parked out front, I came up to see what was wrong." He continued to look around. "You say it was a break-in?"

They nodded.

"I'll keep an eye out. I don't want my tenants put in any danger." The owner shook his head. "When am I going to be able to rent this place?"

Both detectives glared at the man. He backed up and raised his hand. "Hey, I'll give the lady until the end of the month." He disappeared out the door.

The detectives turned to her. "How did you get in here?" Detective Sandoval asked.

"My daughter has a key. When I got Peter's things from the cops, his car keys and his house key weren't among them. His wallet was also missing," said Lilly.

Detective Littledeer's eyes darkened. "I'll go back over the incident report and see if I can locate those keys."

"Detectives, we're done here," one of the evidence techs informed them.

"I can now go through Pete's things?" asked Lilly.

"You can. If you find anything you think would shed light on what happened, call." Detective Littledeer gave her his business card.

"Thanks," she said as the detectives filed out the door behind the techs.

Once alone in the apartment, Lilly scanned the mess. "Oh, Lord, what was Peter into?"

After spending a few hours trying to restore order in Peter's apartment, Lilly drove to her little house a block from San Mateo Street Community Church. Having a job so close to home was a blessing because

Penny could walk to the church after school and help her with the garden. She was the secretary, manager and community gardener for their parish. The garden had started with the pastor wanting to reach out to the community. They'd only had a few of the church ladies help with the planting that first year. Since then it had taken off. This season they'd tripled the amount they harvested from the garden.

She hit the remote for the garage door and waited for the door to open. She would be sure to gather some flowers from her garden to thank Allison for keeping Penny overnight. Allison would probably spoil both the girls with hot-fudge sundaes and let them stay up until nine-thirty. Penny needed spoiling. It had been a rough week for both of them. Once school started next week, hopefully life could return to some semblance of normal. Lilly had hoped the time Penny spent with her would reassure her daughter that she wouldn't leave, too.

Lilly had called her parents in Florida, letting them know what had happened. Her dad hadn't been too sympathetic. Her father never forgave Peter for abandoning his daughter.

Gathering her purse, she got out of the car. She'd boxed Peter's shoes, clothes and dishes. She could give some of the things to several needy families in the church. Opening the door that led into the kitchen, she put her purse on the table and flipped on the light.

She gasped as she looked at the mess in her kitchen. Someone had been in here, searching for…what?

Grabbing her purse, she looked for Jonathan Little-deer's business card. She found it and dialed the number.

"Littledeer."

"Detective, this is Lilly Burkstrom. I just walked into my house. It looks like my husband's apartment wasn't the only place ransacked."

"Your house was broken into?"

"Yes."

A crash from the bedroom made her gasp.

"Lilly."

"I heard something."

"Get out. Go next door and call 911."

She turned and ran out the garage.

TWO

The instant he hung up with Lilly Burkstrom, Jonathan Littledeer called his partner and told him about the incident.

"I can be there in fifteen minutes," Dave told him.

"No." Jon had been reluctant to contact his partner since Dave was celebrating his twins' tenth birthday. "Today is your daughters' birthday. Do not leave that party. If there's anything significant, I'll let you know."

Dave didn't reply. They both knew the reason why Jon wasn't celebrating with the Sandoval family. Jon had lost both of his daughters to a rare genetic disorder—Niemann-Pick disease type C. Both Jon and his wife, Roberta, carried the recessive gene. No one had known the children had the disease until the oldest, Wendy, was two and a half. Rose had been born just a few months before Wendy got sick. She had run a high temperature and had her first seizure. When she had a second seizure after recovering from the fever, the doctors were stumped. It took a while before they were able to determine what was happening. Wendy's body eventually wasted away and she died two days before her fourth birthday. A month after they buried Wendy, Rose had her first seizure. She died much quicker. She suffered for only thirteen months. The day they buried his sweet Rose, Jon's wife went home after the funeral and took too many sleeping pills. Jon buried his wife one week after his youngest daughter was laid to rest.

The next six months were a blur. He was drunk most of the time. The first time he shown up at work drunk, his captain suspended him. Captain Morse blistered the paint off the wall with his words and told him to clean up his act or resign.

One night after a particularly bad binge, Jon showed up at Dave's house, railing. Most of the details of what happened were hazy, but he remembered crying and blaming God for what had happened. How Dave calmed him down, he didn't know, but when Jon surfaced the next morning from his liquor-induced sleep, Caren, one of the twins, was standing over him. She cupped his cheek and softly pronounced that Jesus could heal his hurt.

Those sweet words rolled around in his head for weeks, until Jon went with Dave to church. Caren had been right. Jon gave his heart to Christ and started down the road to healing. Some things, such as the girls' birthday, he had to skip, but his life was so much better. More than once, God had brought people into his life that he could comfort in the same way he'd been comforted.

The night he'd told Lilly Burkstrom of her ex-husband's murder stood out in his mind. She'd collapsed in a chair and, although the man was her ex, Jon had seen her honest grief. But what had nearly brought him to his knees was when Penny came into the room and learned of her father's death.

What he'd seen in Lilly's eyes as she comforted her daughter had reached into his heart and touched him. He couldn't figure out if it was her strength in comforting her daughter or if it was the pain in her eyes when she'd met his gaze. There was an understanding there, a shared sorrow. Pain. He didn't know what to do with this understanding, but he found himself thinking of Lilly at odd times. Something had sparked between them, making him jumpy. He knew the Lord could use him to comfort others, but heaven knew that he didn't want another relationship. He would be the forever bachelor.

Pulling up to Lilly Burkstrom's house, he saw her sitting on a bench by the front walk. He parked behind the patrol car and got out.

She stood, brushing off her pants. "The patrolman just got here. He's looking through the house."

Stepping to her side, he asked, "So you don't know how someone got into the house?"

"No. The front door was locked when I got home."

He nodded. "I'll go inside and see what's going on."

"Thanks."

Jon moved into the house and surveyed the living room. It wasn't in as much disarray as Peter Burkstrom's apartment had been in, but the drawers of the coffee table were open and the cushions on the couch were out of alignment. He moved through the dining area and into the kitchen. Drawers hung open and cabinet doors stood ajar.

He heard someone behind him. He turned and saw the uniformed officer, Miguel Aguilar. "What are you doing here, Littledeer? I haven't seen any bodies."

"The lady's ex-husband was murdered last week. She called me before she dialed 911. Earlier, the ex's apartment was broken into and trashed. This place is in better shape, but… How's the rest of the house?"

"It's been tossed."

"Any indication where the perpetrator got in?"

"The sliding glass door in the master bedroom was jimmied. It has one of those cheap locks."

"You call for the evidence team?"

"Yeah. They're on the way."

He moved through the rest of the house. Whoever had broken in had been more careful than they'd been at Peter's apartment. It sure seemed as if someone was after something—which led him to believe Lilly's assertion that maybe her ex-husband's death wasn't the random event they thought it might be.

As he turned to leave the master bedroom, he noticed the framed picture on the dresser. It had been knocked on its side. He picked up the frame. Penny, who was maybe twelve or thirteen months old at the time, sat on her mother's lap. They were both smiling. It was the kind of picture that any husband or grandparent would view with joy and pride.

He remembered the picture of Roberta, Wendy and Rose on his mantel at home. It had been taken right before they knew the killing truth. Wendy had been two and a half; Rose two months. It was a picture he hadn't been able to look at since he'd buried Roberta.

He carefully replaced the picture and walked back outside. Lilly and an unknown woman quietly talked. When Lilly saw him, she ushered the woman toward him.

"This is my neighbor, Sandra Tillman. She thought she saw someone in the house," Lilly explained.

"What did you see?" Jon asked.

The woman rubbed her arms. "When I went out to bring in Lucky, my dog, I saw a light flash inside Lilly's house. I stopped and watched. The light never appeared again, so I shrugged it off as my imagination, but seeing the patrol car, I thought I'd tell Lilly what I saw."

"Did you see a car near the house? Or anyone leave?" he asked.

The woman shook her head. "Sorry." The slump of her shoulders gave away her disappointment at not being able to provide more information.

"Thank you for your help. I wish more people would step up to the plate. What you've told me is that the man, assuming it is a man and he worked alone, might have parked his car on the next street over. I'll be sure to question the neighbors on that street."

The woman's spine straightened. "I'll keep my eyes open." She turned and walked back to her house.

"That was nice of you," Lilly whispered to him.

"No, it wasn't. It was the truth. I know where to look for the suspect."

She turned, her brow raised.

"You doubt me? You think I wasn't sincere?"

"I guess I hadn't thought—"

"Littledeer, I'm done," one of the evidence guys interrupted. "I'll be sure to check for what you asked." He moved down the sidewalk to his car.

"What did you ask him to do?" Lilly asked Jon.

"To compare the prints he lifted here and at your ex-husband's apartment. And remember, we'll need your and Penny's prints."

"You think it was the same person?" Fear tinged her voice.

He didn't want to panic her, but she needed to know. "I don't know, but I don't want to overlook anything." She didn't need to dwell on the fear. "C'mon. Let's go inside and fix your sliding glass door."

"You don't need—"

"That's what cops do, help make the public safe. Now, if you know how to secure that door, I'll leave it for you."

"You win. I have to beg my friend to come over and fix things." Shaking her head, she confided, "Zoe is one handy lady. She's working at the local home improvement store while she puts herself through college."

"I'm impressed."

They walked through the living room and into her bedroom. The lock on the sliding glass door was a simple lever, which opened when turned to the right.

"It's not broken," Lilly said.

"True, but it's easily opened. A slim blade here—" he pointed above the lock and motioned downward "—and the intruder's inside." He looked around the room, then walked out, thinking he could find what he needed in the kitchen. In the pantry, he found a broom. He brought it back into the bedroom. Holding it up, he asked, "You willing to sacrifice this for your safety?"

"Yes."

He snapped the broom handle over his knee and placed the piece without the bristles in the door's track. "That will do until you decide what other locking mechanism you want for the door. Zoe will know what other safety measures are out there. Oh, one of the officers secured the sliding glass doors in the living room, but you'll need to buy new locks for those doors, too."

"Thank you." Turning, she glanced around the room. "At least it's not as bad as Pete's." After a moment, she dashed out of the room.

He followed her into Penny's room. It had been ransacked, too.

"Who did this? And why?" She picked up a stuffed doll and buried her face in the doll's chest. She'd held it together through the mess at her ex-husband's apartment and the mess here.

He moved to her side. "Lilly."

She turned into his arms and the dam broke. She wrapped one arm around his waist and the other clutched the doll between them. His arms closed around her shoulders. The emotions tumbling around his chest he didn't want to name, but he knew that feelings he'd thought long dead had come back to life.

Slowly, the storm of tears and fears faded. She felt safe being held in this man's strong arms. When he looked at her, she thought she saw something responding to her in those deep brown eyes.

She wiped away the tear hanging off her chin. She looked and noticed the wet spot on the shirt covering Jon Littledeer's chest.

"Oh," she said, jerking backward. "I'm so sorry."

He released her and looked down into her face. "It's understandable. You've been through a lot."

"I meant messing up your shirt."

His gaze moved to his shirt, then back to her face. His lips turned up into the slightest smile. "It's wash and wear."

She couldn't look at him. "That's good." Looking at the doll, she added, "He is, too." Her gaze roamed the room. "I'll have to clean this up before Penny gets back. It's too much for her to handle."

She started to put the doll in the toy box. Amazingly, Jon picked up another doll.

"Detective, you don't have to do that."

"Call me Jon."

"But—"

He glanced down at his shirt. The wet spot seemed to glow in the light. "I don't allow just anyone to leave wet spots on my shirt." His smile encouraged her to relax.

She returned his smile. "Okay."

As they worked to put things right in Penny's room, Jon said, "What do you think your ex-husband meant when he told you his death wouldn't be an accident?"

"I don't know. After our divorce Pete dropped by occasionally. I don't think anyone knew where he spent most of his time."

"You think he was into illegal things?"

"I don't know. He never said what he'd been doing or where he'd been."

"Do you think he told anyone in his family?"

"His parents are dead, and I don't know anyone else in his family." She closed the final drawer of her daughter's dresser.

"You know nothing of his family?"

"No. When we were in high school, his parents were killed in a car accident. Afterward, he lived with his neighbors until he graduated from high school." With a sigh, she walked out of Penny's room. "One down and four more rooms to go."

"Let's tackle that living room. I have more questions to ask."

Straightening up wasn't that bad. It had been a long day and she couldn't face that mess by herself. The help was a godsend.

They got to work in the living room, putting the furniture back in place.

"Tell me about you and Peter," Jon said after a while.

"As I told you, I knew Pete in high school. It was during my sophomore year at the University of New Mexico that I ran into him again. He'd transferred from

New Mexico Highlands University to UNM. We started dating and fell in love. We married over the Christmas holidays. Around Easter I discovered I was pregnant. When we came home from the university that summer, he told me he didn't want to be a father and wanted a divorce. He disappeared, never went back to school. Suddenly, marriage was a prison and he couldn't breathe. I stayed with my parents and went to the community college."

She pushed in the last cushion on the couch and sat. "I didn't understand why he didn't want our baby. After our divorce I saw him infrequently. Where he'd been or what he'd been doing, I don't know." She didn't want to face those memories. Pushing off the couch, she walked into the kitchen.

Jon followed her. "What do you know about Peter after he got his life in order?"

"He started working for a construction company, building roads and bridges here in the state. I think he helped with some bridges in Colorado and Arizona. Sometimes he'd be gone for months at a time, but he'd faithfully call Penny on Mondays and Wednesdays. He'd come home every other week and spend time with her."

Jon helped put the scattered cans back into the pantry as she put the kitchen drawers in order. "What was he doing around the time he died?"

"He'd gone back to school. He'd also started going to church again." She remembered the happiness that had filled her heart when he'd come to know Jesus.

She'd wanted to shout for joy. By then she and Peter had come to love each other as brother and sister.

"What are you not telling me?" Jon asked, sitting on a stool under the high counter.

"Are you married, Jon?"

He looked as if she'd slapped him. "Not any— No."

There was so much in that no. For an instant she saw pain and grief.

"It's odd, but I thought of Pete as a brother. It took me a while to get over the hurt, but God turned Pete and me around and healed our relationship. Both of us wanted what was best for Penny."

Leaning forward, he rested his elbows on the counter. "Did he mention problems at work with coworkers and his boss?"

She settled next to Jon on the other stool. "He just recently changed jobs, but I think that had more to do with wanting to go back to school than anything else." She stared down at the counter. "I think he wanted to stay here for Penny."

"Do you think his job had anything to do with the murder?"

"I don't know. He had just started driving an armored car for Sunbelt Securities."

"And there were no problems there?"

"He didn't mention anything. The only thing that he said was money was heavy. You could talk to his co-workers. They were at the funeral."

He nodded. Glancing around the kitchen, he said, "I think you're good to go."

They'd managed to clean up the house in less than forty minutes. Her stomach growled. He grinned.

"I haven't eaten. Cleaning up Peter's place, I didn't have time."

His cell phone rang. "Littledeer here." He shook his head. "I'm okay, Marta. No, no." He glanced at Lilly and shook his head again. "Yes, you are right. Okay, I'll come for cake. You have anything left to eat?" After a moment he added, "Good. Because I haven't eaten and I'm bringing another hungry person with me." He listened to the response, then hung up. "You've been invited to a birthday dinner. Want to come?"

She started to refuse, but saw something in Jon's eyes that she recognized as a well-hidden pain. Besides, she didn't want to stay here by herself. Not yet.

"You driving?

He smiled. "You bet."

"Then I'm coming."

"Just be prepared to be grilled unmercifully by two of the best," he warned her as they got into his car.

"What are you talking about?" She couldn't keep the hint of panic out of her voice.

"Twin ten-year-old girls."

He said it with such sincerity that she wanted to laugh.

"I think I can handle that."

He snorted.

"Did you find anything?" the older man demanded. He sat behind the desk like a king or president.

"Not at the first place. I did a thorough search. It wasn't there."

"What about his ex's place?"

Running his hands over his short hair, the younger man said, "She showed up too soon. I wasn't able to finish looking for what you want." He walked across the room and looked out the window to the street ten stories below. The streetlights made it easier to see his car parked in the alley below. "If you want another search, it will cost you."

The older man darted around his desk and charged across the room. "I pay for results. You got me nothing."

The younger man didn't like being threatened. "I'm not the one whose life will go in the dumper if that information is found."

The older man's eyes narrowed. "No, but you'll have done the crime without being paid."

"I can walk away anytime." He turned and walked to the door.

"Okay, okay," the older man huffed, adjusting his attitude. "Get me the proof and I'll double your fee to ten thousand."

The younger man nodded and left the other man standing in the middle of the room. He wasn't the one who'd go the jail. Mr. Self-Importance would. He wouldn't go to jail again for anyone. If Mr. Self-Importance wouldn't take the fall voluntarily, his death would solve the problem.

THREE

When they walked into the Pizza Palace, it wasn't hard to spot the twins. Once the twins got a look at Jon, they raced across the room, dodging tables and people, and threw themselves at him.

He scooped the girls into his arms and kissed each one. They giggled.

"Uncle Jon, I'm so glad you came," Caren declared as she kissed him on the cheek. She glanced over his shoulder. "Who's the lady?" she asked in a stage whisper.

"She's a lady who is hungry. Show me where the pizza is," he replied.

"On the table," said Caren.

Connie, the other twin, looked over his shoulder and smiled at Lilly. "Hi."

"Happy birthday," Lilly said.

"I'm the older one," Connie informed her.

"Yeah, but I'm the smarter one," Caren countered.

He heard Lilly laugh.

As they approached the party table, Dave stood. Jon saw the question in his eyes.

After the introductions were made, Jon pulled Dave aside and told him what he'd found at Lilly's house.

"Gives credence to what she said earlier about his death not being an accident," David observed. "The search of both her and her ex's place says someone's looking for something. But what?"

"I don't know, but it gives this case a different angle from what we thought, Dave. I think we're going to have to look at the victim much more closely."

Dave glanced at Lilly. "You think she's involved in any way with Peter's murder?"

Jon remembered her reaction to the break-ins, and her words earlier about Peter going back to church. "I don't think so." He had that gut feeling cops got when interviewing witnesses and suspects that told them if someone was telling the truth. "So far there's no evidence pointing in any way to her."

Dave sighed. "There's no evidence for anything, Jon. These break-ins occurred out of the blue. You know that. We have to go back to square one and look at everything again."

"I know."

Dave pinned him with a look. "Is there something you're not telling me?"

"No." But there was, his heart yelled.

Dave held Jon's gaze.

"She was hungry. I was hungry." Jon glanced at the twins, then met Dave's gaze. He didn't say anything, but let Dave see his pain. Jon missed his girls and having Lilly here helped.

Dave clapped him on the back. "Let's go join the party."

"You married?" Caren asked as she took a bite of her pizza. Her big brown eyes held Lilly's.

"Caren," Marta, Dave's wife, gasped. Her daughter peeked at her mother.

"That's okay," Lilly assured Marta.

Marta glared at her daughter. "It isn't any business of yours."

Caren put down her piece of pizza. "I just wanted to make sure she's not married. I don't want Uncle Jon to get hurt anymore."

Both women stared at her.

Caren went on. "He's been so sad. His girls died, you know. They were sick. And his wife died of a broken heart. Uncle Jon used to drink and come to the house and fall asleep on the couch. I don't want to see him sad anymore."

Marta's cheeks heated. "I'm glad you love your uncle Jon, but I don't think your uncle wants you telling people about that time."

Caren thought a moment, then nodded. "He's been better since he began going to church with us." She leaned close to Lilly. "Mom and Dad told us that sometimes he's real sad, like on our birthday. That's why he didn't come join us earlier. But I'm glad you made him come."

Marta and Lilly sat at the table, stunned into silence.

"Do you have a husband?" Connie asked. She sat on the other side of her mother.

The other twin's question snapped Lilly out of her shock. "Not anymore."

The girls traded looks.

"I do have a daughter," Lilly quickly added to ward off another uncomfortable question. "I think you'd like her. She sometimes works with me at our church's community garden. You should visit."

Jon and Dave walked back to the table and sat down.

"What are you ladies talking about?" Jon asked.

Silence greeted his question.

"So you work in the community garden at your church?" Marta asked, ignoring Jon's question.

Grateful to change the subject, Lilly answered, "I do. I direct the whole gardening operation. It's turned out to be a wonderful blessing to the neighbors. It's fun to observe the kids from the area plant vegetables and then watch as they grow. The kids are so surprised when we pull a carrot out of the ground. Or when they see a tomato appear on a vine. They thought carrots and tomatoes came from the supermarket."

"Don't they?" Connie asked.

All four adults paused.

"They grow in the ground or on a vine first, then are harvested and sent to grocery stores," Lilly explained.

"Is that true?" Caren asked her father.

Trying to hide his smile, Dave said, "Yes."

Lilly leaned close to Caren. "The kids even love eating those carrots."

Doubt colored Caren's eyes. "You sure?"

Lilly nodded. "I am. Come down anytime and see the garden. You can even come to the garden and help pull the carrots or harvest the tomatoes yourself. I know my daughter loves to come to the garden and harvest vegetables. It's work, but it's fun and you'll enjoy it."

The twins glanced at each other. "Okay," they said in unison.

Lilly smiled at Jon. From his expression, she could tell that he wasn't satisfied with her answer to what they were talking about. She didn't want him to know they'd been talking about his wife and daughters.

Jon studied each girl. Caren calmly ate her pizza, the corners of her mouth turned up in a smile. Connie giggled as she ate.

"It's a girl thing," Lilly whispered. "You don't want to know what we were talking about."

Jon cocked his head.

"The pizza's good. Try some," Lilly said.

After a few moments, Jon shrugged and started eating pizza.

As the evening progressed, the twins retreated to the restaurant's video game arcade. They pulled Jon from one machine to the next. He was happy to help bowl on a screen or drive a digital car.

"Mom, Mom, c'mon," Caren called.

Marta joined her daughters.

Dave studied Lilly, who was still sitting at the table.

"I'm sure the girls asked you a million questions about your personal life. I hope the girls haven't offended you."

She shrugged. "They're just curious."

"Speaking of girls, your daughter wasn't with you at your house, was she?"

"No, I let her stay with my cousin after what happened at Pete's place."

He nodded and looked at his partner.

"I didn't ask Jon to bring me here tonight," she added, trying to reassure Dave.

His gaze returned to her. Sighing, he glanced down at the table. "I believe you."

"You do?"

"Yeah. He loves the girls, but—"

She nodded her head.

"They told you about his family, huh?"

"Caren wanted to make sure I wouldn't hurt her uncle Jon. They love him and are very protective."

The love Dave had for his daughters shone in his eyes. "My little warriors." He shook his head. "Jon's been through a lot. I didn't think he'd make it. God reached down and sent a little angel, Caren, to get him to church. She might be a missionary when she grows up."

"What are you doing?" Marta asked, sitting next to her husband.

"Finding out what caring children I have."

Jon parked his car in front of Lilly's house. He turned off the engine and got out.

"You don't have to walk me to the door," Lilly said, climbing out of the front seat.

"I do, and I'd like to make sure that everything inside is okay."

She nodded and he thought he saw relief in her eyes. Unlocking the front door, they walked inside. He checked all the windows and the sliding glass door in her bedroom.

"You probably should also get window locks. They are very simple to install and will prevent anyone from opening a window," he said as they entered the living room. "They rest in the track, then the window can only be opened up to the lock. If someone wants in, they can't force the window up and the only alternative is to break the glass. Most thieves won't do that. They need secrecy and breaking glass won't provide that."

"I'll buy those tomorrow."

He looked around her house one last time. "After thinking about it, has anything else occurred to you as to why someone would break into your place and your ex-husband's place?"

"No. This was my parents' place. When Dad and Mom moved to Florida, they let me buy it from them. I work for San Mateo Street Community Church. I've been there for almost eight years. There is nothing here in this house that someone would want. My TVs are almost ten years old and my daughter doesn't have any computer games."

He nodded. "Call me if you can think of anything."

As he drove home, he realized that going to the twins' birthday party had been an enjoyable experience. He wondered what had been different this time.

* * *

Jon walked into the squad room. "What do you have?" he asked Dave, who sat behind his desk.

"Well, I've run a credit check on our victim. He didn't spend wildly. He paid his bills and drove a five-year-old pickup. He got paid well for driving the armored car." Looking up, Dave added, "I think I might be in the wrong business. I know Marta would like a little more take-home pay in my envelope."

Jon ignored his partner's comment. Dave wouldn't trade being a cop for three times the pay. "Did Peter Burkstrom have any saving accounts that we know of?" Jon asked.

"Nothing at any bank here in Albuquerque."

"It's time that we started interviewing his old bosses and his last colleagues."

"Let's go," Dave replied.

Their first stop was Sunbelt Securities. Dave's team and their armored car were on their route. Jon and Dave were told to come back around four in the afternoon.

"They seemed mighty unfriendly," Dave grumbled as he climbed into the passenger seat of the patrol car.

"I noticed that, too. Be interesting to see if Peter's colleagues are warned about the pending interview with us." Jon pulled out into traffic. "Let's make a little trip to our victim's apartment. Maybe someone saw something. Or knows something."

As they drove to the apartment complex on the

west side of the city, they passed by San Mateo Street Community Church. The garden took up an entire side of the church and wrapped around the back of the main structure.

Dave nodded toward the garden. "The girls want to see this garden. They talked about it all the way home after the party."

Jon threw him a startled look. "Really? You're telling me that Miss Caren, who can't stand any dirt on her person, who doesn't want to play outside because she might get dirty, wants to garden?"

"That's what I'm saying. It made me shake my head in disbelief. Marta questioned her about it, warned her about the dirt, but she wants to visit the garden. Connie wants to see it, too."

"That's easier to believe." Of the two twins, Connie was the more adventurous. She was the one who, at nineteen months old, found a bug in the backyard and ate it. Granted, she was a toddler when it happened, but of the two girls, Connie was the daredevil.

Jon turned into the Mission apartment complex. They knocked on the doors of several of the apartments around Peter Burkstrom's place. At the third apartment, a young woman answered the door. After they identified themselves, Jon asked, "How well did you know Peter Burkstrom?"

"I moved into my place about seven months ago," the woman said. "I'd just moved here from Dumas, a little town in the Texas Panhandle, and didn't know anyone. Pete helped me move in."

"Were you close?" Dave asked.

She shrugged. "We were friendly, but we didn't date, if that's what you're asking." She leaned close. "He was a little too old for me."

Dave threw Jon a grin.

"No, that's not what we wanted to know," said Jon. "Did anything unusual happen around here recently, anything involving Mr. Burkstrom? Any falling-out with neighbors, fights? Or was he acting strangely?"

She thought for several minutes and said, "You know, about a month ago, I saw Pete arguing with a man out in the parking lot. I thought they were going to start throwing punches, but then the other guy pointed his finger at Peter, said something, turned around and disappeared around the corner of the apartment building. I saw a dark green car drive out a minute later. It was a very expensive car."

"Do you remember the license plate?" asked Dave.

She shook her head. "But it was a luxury convertible. Black. It's my dream car."

Jon handed her a business card. "If you think of anything else or see anything suspicious, call us."

She took the card and put it in a front pocket of her jeans. Jon and Dave finished canvassing the area. No one else answered their knock.

Checking his watch, Jon said, "Let's stop by Sunbelt Securities and see if that armored car is back."

"A little earlier than planned? You want to catch them off guard?"

The best way to catch people covering up evidence

was showing up unexpectedly. They wanted to see if anyone at the armored car company needed to hide something.

"Let's go," Jon said.

"Mom, Mom," Penny yelled, running toward Lilly, who rolled up the garden hose. "Can I go home with Ann? Her mom says we can swim this afternoon and then make snow cones."

Tuesdays were the days that Ann and her mom helped in the church garden. When Lilly was first hired as the church's secretary, manager and gardener by the new young pastor, he told her he wanted to reach out to the neighborhood. He'd come up with the idea to use the side yard of the church for a community garden.

The garden's success had stunned all of them. Young couples from the neighborhood helped with the garden, then started coming to church. Ann and her parents lived close to the church and helped regularly with the garden. At the end of the growing season, they passed out fresh vegetables to the neighbors. It had been a wonderful ministry. And it had brought many people into the church who had heard about Jesus.

"You're going to desert me?" Lilly asked her daughter. "And I'm not going to get a snow cone?"

Penny laughed. "I bet you could come and have snow cones with us." She looked over her shoulder at her friend.

Ann's mom stood behind her daughter. "Since they worked so hard today, I thought an afternoon in the pool was what they needed."

"Can I, Mom?" Penny turned on her acting ability and played a poor, deserving soul.

Lilly nodded. "Okay, but—"

The girls' shrieks filled the air.

"You don't have your bathing suit," Lilly said.

Penny's expression fell.

"Ann has several suits," Ann's mom said. "Penny can use one of them."

Her father's death had knocked Penny for a loop. This was the first time since Peter's death that Lilly had seen her daughter excited. "Okay."

Penny hugged her mother's waist. "You're the best, Mom."

"I'll be at Ann's house at six," Lilly said.

"Okay," Penny agreed. The girls bounced around.

"You can have my new suit," Ann told Penny as they walked away.

Ann's mom walked behind the girls, shaking her head.

With her daughter occupied this afternoon, Lilly could go to Peter's apartment and continue packing his things up.

After letting the pastor know where she was going, she left the church. The drive to Peter's place took less than ten minutes.

She'd talked with Pastor Kent about what to do with Peter's things. He'd found several needy families in the parish that could use clothes, dishes and a television.

All she needed to do was go through Peter's things and see what she might want to save for Penny.

She pulled into the parking lot of the apartment complex and found a spot near Peter's apartment. Pulling boxes out of the backseat, she wrestled them up the stairs. She fumbled with Penny's key and dropped it. Picking it up, she unlocked the door and dragged the boxes into the living room. As she turned around, she spotted a man hiding behind the door.

Before she could yell, his fist shot out, hitting her on the chin, and darkness descended.

FOUR

Something gnawed at his gut. Jon flexed his hands on the steering wheel of their police-issue sedan, trying to sort through the tension. He'd learned a long time ago not to ignore his instincts.

"What is it?" Dave asked.

Jon threw his partner a glance. "What?"

"You've got that look."

He could try to deny it, but Dave and Jon had been partners long enough to read each other's body language. "Something's wrong."

"Well, that clears things up."

"You've followed hunches, and I've not complained," Jon retorted.

"Yeah."

"Before we pay Sunbelt a surprise visit, let's run back to Peter's apartment. Maybe we need to talk to the manager about that incident the neighbor mentioned. See if he has a tape of the incident."

Dave didn't hesitate or complain. "Let's go."

Jon turned the car around and headed toward Peter's

place. It was only a couple of streets away from their current position.

When they arrived at the apartment complex, Jon spotted Lilly's car parked in the lot. Suddenly a man ran out of Peter's second-story apartment and raced toward the stairs.

Jon slammed the car into Park, jerked the keys out of the ignition, and both men ran toward the stairs. The man spotted them, turned on the stairs and ran back up them. On the second floor, he darted in the opposite direction from Peter's place.

"I've got him," Dave yelled, reaching the second-floor landing.

Jon raced up the steps and to the open door of Peter's apartment. "Lilly," he yelled.

Inside the door, he saw Lilly sprawled on the floor. He knelt by her side and swept a glance over her body. She didn't have any obvious wounds, and there was no blood. It was a good sign, but he'd encountered more than one murder victim who had died of internal injuries. Carefully, he ran his hands over her torso and limbs, searching for any hidden wounds. Finding nothing to cause him alarm, he ran his hands over her head. She wasn't bleeding, but he noticed the red welt on her chin.

"Lilly, wake up." He gently ran his hands through her hair.

She moaned. Jon welcomed the sound.

"C'mon, Lilly. Open your eyes." He brushed away the hair from her face.

Her eyes fluttered open.

He let out the breath that he'd been holding. *Thank You, Lord,* he thought.

"Are you hurt anywhere?" he asked in a quiet voice.

She tried to focus on his face. He saw her struggle to make sense of things. Finally, things snapped into place. "My jaw feels like an elephant sat on it." She tried to smile, but winced instead.

She struggled to sit up. Jon helped her.

"What happened?" he asked.

"I came to finish packing up Pete's clothes and things. When I opened the door and stepped into the living room, a man appeared behind me and punched. That's the last thing I remember." She tried to get up.

Jon caught her arm, helping her to stand. He directed her to a kitchen chair. "Take a moment to gather yourself."

"How is she?" Dave asked from the doorway. Jon glanced at his partner. Dave shook his head, letting Jon know that the suspect had got away. He motioned to Lilly. "Is she okay?"

"I'm fine. I just got punched in the face," Lilly answered. She moved her jaw and winced.

Jon went to the refrigerator and removed several ice cubes from the ice bin. He took a kitchen towel, wrapped the ice cubes in it and brought it over to Lilly. "Here. Put that on your chin."

She took the towel and followed his suggestion. "What does the guy who did this to me want?" she asked after a minute.

That was the burning question that Jon was mulling. "Obviously, whoever he is, he's looking for something he hasn't yet found, and he came back to look for it again."

"I don't understand." She put the towel on the table. "Pete doesn't have anything worth taking."

"You sure?" Dave asked. "He wasn't into anything illegal?"

Lilly shook her head. "I don't know. But it wouldn't make sense given the fact that there were so many signs that he took his faith seriously. Penny commented recently that her daddy had started reading her children's Bible to her when she spent the weekends."

Jon pointed to the towel with the ice and pointed at her chin. "Keep it on your face. You don't want Penny to see her mom with a huge bruise on her face."

She obeyed and placed the towel on her chin again.

Jon sat down at the table. "Whoever was in here today, yesterday, and at your house yesterday is looking for something. We need to figure out what it is, because it looks like this guy isn't going to quit until he gets what he wants. Do you have any idea what this person is looking for?"

Worry colored Lilly's eyes, turning them deep chocolate. "I don't know."

Jon placed his hand over hers. The electricity that ran up his arm shocked him. He pulled his hand back. "Can you call someone to come and help you with things here at the apartment? I'd feel a lot better if someone was here with you. And I know Penny would appreciate it, too."

He got the smile out of her that he wanted.

"Who can you call?" Jon asked, pressing the matter. They weren't leaving until someone was here with Lilly.

"I can ask the pastor to come and help me. And he knows several people who would gladly help."

"Then do that. Dave and I will stay here until someone arrives."

"You don't have to do that," she protested.

"I do." Jon's tone made it clear that he would brook no argument. "Remember the condition of your house?"

He had a point. They didn't know what was going on and until they did, there was danger.

"You got security cameras?" Jon asked Mark Rodgers, the owner and manager of the apartment complex.

"There are a couple in the parking lot, but the security tapes are erased after a couple of weeks."

"Let us have what you've got," said Jon.

Rodgers hesitated. "You going to bring them back?" Jon glared at him.

Rodgers shrugged. "Hey, they're expensive."

"File it with the insurance company," Dave told him.

Rodgers didn't look happy, but he walked back into his office. He reappeared a few minutes later with seven tapes. "I use one a day and have one for each day of the week."

"If you keep two weeks worth of tape, how come you only have seven tapes?" Jon asked.

"Because, the tapes are not on all the time. I have

the tapes running only when the tenants go to work and come home," Rodgers explained.

It wasn't an uncommon practice. They'd be lucky if the argument Peter had in the parking lot was caught on tape, but miracles still did happen.

"Hey, do I get a receipt for those tapes?" Rodgers asked.

Jon stepped into Rodger's office, looked around the man's desk, saw an envelope, turned it on its back and wrote a receipt.

"That's my electric bill," Rogers complained from the doorway.

"It's also your receipt. Don't lose it." Jon slapped it down on the desk.

Jon and Dave headed for the patrol car.

"You've got to work on your technique," Dave muttered, trying to hide his smile.

Jon threw him a look. "He wants his tapes back?"

"We've heard stranger things."

Jon tried to fit the pieces of this case together as he sat behind the wheel without turning the key. "The more we look into Burkstrom's murder, the more sense Lilly's words make. I mean about her husband warning her about his death." Jon glanced at his partner, wondering if they were on the same page.

"You're right. There seem to be red flags popping up everywhere."

"Let's go to Sunbelt and see if anyone knows a reason why Burkstrom was murdered."

It took only ten minutes to drive to the offices of

Sunbelt Securities. One of the managers, Bryon Sands, whom they'd talked to earlier, looked up from his desk.

"Detectives? Aren't you early?" He glanced at his watch. "The guys are still out on their run."

"We thought we might stop by and see if the team might've finished earlier," Jon explained.

Bryon Sands stood and walked to the counter separating the desks from the lobby. "Car fourteen isn't back yet. They're still out doing their morning run."

"Aren't they running a little late?" Jon asked. "One-thirty is late for a lunch break."

Sands glanced down at his watch again. "It is, but sometimes our customers run late or change their mind. The team radioed in and told us they were about a half hour behind their normal schedule. I've radioed their morning clients about the delay."

"Since that team is going to be late, we'd like to interview some of the other teams and see if they can tell us anything," Jon announced.

Sands didn't look happy. "Sure. Drive around back and talk to whomever you need to."

The detectives walked back to their car.

Dave met Jon's gaze over the roof of the car. "We have a reluctant boss. Why?"

"I wonder if we'll get to talk to all the team members," Jon replied. They glanced around the lot. An armored car drove in and pulled into the garage. "Maybe we should check out who is on that team."

"I like your thinking."

The detectives walked around the building to the

garage. Several armored cars were parked at the loading dock and inside the garage. They could hear the
men joking with each other. Jon and Dave walked up
the concrete steps to the loading dock. One of the men
looked up and his hand went to his sidearm.

"We're Albuquerque police detectives," Jon offered
to disarm the situation. He pulled out his police ID and
showed it to the man.

The man let his arm drop.

Jon said, "We're here to ask a few questions about
Peter Burkstrom."

"He worked here only a couple of months," the
man offered.

"And he wasn't on our team," another man replied.
He sat on a wooden box. Several other boxes had been
pulled up to an old table. Three other men sat around
the table. A couple of men stood behind it.

"We realize that," said Dave. "But we wanted to see
if any of you might recall some incident where Peter
might have had a problem with someone?"

Jon stood back and carefully watched the reactions
of the men. Most of the men shook their heads, but
one man in the back shoved his hands into his pock-
ets. He didn't offer any explanation, but Jon wanted
to talk to him.

Jon and Dave pulled each of the men aside to talk
to them privately. The third man Jon interviewed was
the man who had aroused his suspicions.

"Do you know anyone who might've had something against Burkstrom?" Jon asked.

The man hesitated.

"If you know anything, no matter how insignificant, tell me. It might be the key to Pete's death."

"About a month ago, Pete had a bad argument with one of his team members."

"Who was that?"

"His name is Jimmy Hughes. When they got back from a run, Jimmy jumped all over Pete, calling him stupid and saying that if 'that' happened again, he would report Pete to the office."

"You don't know what the argument was about?" Jon asked, pressing.

"No, and when I tried to talk to Pete about it, he told me it was nothing and not to worry about it."

"Did anything else happen?"

The man shook his head. "No. I watched Pete and Jimmy after that, but whatever their differences were, they seemed to patch it up."

"Thanks."

The man shrugged and walked away.

Before Jon could talk to Dave, the armored car they'd been waiting for drove up. The team of four men piled out of the vehicle.

"I could eat your and my lunch," one of the men on the team commented.

They walked up the steps and greeted the other men.

"It looks like a funeral in here. What's wrong?" the hungry man commented.

Jon stepped forward. "Detective Sandoval and I are here to talk to you about Pete Burkstrom."

None of the team members who'd just arrived looked happy or willing to talk.

Jon and Dave each took an employee aside and started questioning them.

A few minutes later, Jon studied Jimmy Hughes. "Did you like Peter Burkstrom?"

Jimmy glanced at one of his teammates, who was talking to Dave.

Jon didn't push him. The man had something to say, and he needed the space to say it.

"No." Jimmy looked down at his hands.

"You wanted him dead?"

Jimmy's head jerked up. "No. He was killed in a robbery gone bad."

"Maybe not."

The color drained from Jimmy's face. "You blowing smoke?"

"No, and that's why my partner and I are here, interviewing the people Peter Burkstrom worked with. Some of the guys say you and Pete had a falling-out."

Jimmy raised his index finger and wagged it back and forth. "I objected to that man hanging around this lot. More than once that man questioned me about Pete. I told Pete to get rid of him. No one needs to be hanging around here."

"What happened after that?" Jon asked, pressing.

"Pete must've done something, because the man never showed up here again. I had nothing against Pete. You can ask the other team members. They'll tell you."

"You catch the name of the man after Pete?"

"No. The dude wouldn't ID himself. He'd say, 'Just tell Pete an old friend was asking about him.'"

Jon jotted down Jimmy's statement. "Thanks," he said.

Jimmy nodded his head and moved away with lightning speed.

As they drove away, Jon and Dave compared notes. Several of Peter's teammates had issues with the mystery man. They had a lead, but who was their guy?

Lilly loaded the last of Peter's things in her car. With the help of the pastor and two workers from the church, Jack and Enrique, she'd finished cleaning out Pete's apartment. They'd already left with a load of furniture. Jack and Enrique were going to deliver the things tonight to different people in the church. Lilly had kept several of Peter's things for Penny: his high school yearbooks, pictures of Pete when he was Penny's age, his fishing rod, and the digital frame Peter had put the latest pictures of him and Penny in.

Her cell phone rang. "Hello."

"Hey, Mom. Could I stay for dinner? Ann and her family are going to have barbecue hamburgers and hot dogs."

The hope in her daughter's voice encouraged her. "Let me talk to Ann's mom just to make sure it is okay."

"It is. Mrs. Anderson," Penny bellowed.

"Penny, don't yell. Go get Mrs. Anderson."

"Okay."

Within moments, Lilly had talked with Ann's mom

and settled everything. The Andersons would bring Penny home.

Lilly locked Peter's apartment, turned and ran into Mark Rodgers, the apartment complex's owner and manager. She backed up a step. Something about the man unsettled her.

"Are you finished with the apartment?" he asked. His eyes drilled into her.

"I can finish tomorrow. I thought I'd clean it up and check to make sure nothing was left."

"You won't need to clean it."

"I'd like to get back the deposit."

"Don't worry about it. I'll give it to you."

Lilly wanted to make a search of the place without the distraction of sorting through household clothes and items to determine what she would save and give away. "I need more time in the apartment just to make sure nothing is left behind."

Rodgers held out his hand. "You can hand over the key now."

"Peter's rent is paid up until the end of the month. It's only three more days. I'll give you the key tomorrow after I finish."

His lips pressed together. "Fine. I'll expect to see you tomorrow for the last time." He turned and marched off.

Charm wasn't one of Mr. Rodgers's strong points. Still feeling unsettled, she walked to her car. Why was Rodgers in such a hurry to get into Peter's place? Something wasn't right.

She put the last load of things in the backseat of her car and headed for home. At the first traffic light, she saw the big home improvement store where her old high school friend, Zoe, worked. She needed to stop there and buy those window and door locks Jon had told her about. She hoped Zoe was working tonight.

The instant Lilly walked into the store, she spotted her friend.

"Hey, what are you doing here?" Zoe asked.

"I need to buy locks for the windows of the house and locks for the sliding glass doors."

Zoe straightened. "What's going on?"

Lilly told her what had occurred. "Can you come and help install them tonight?"

"You bet. I'm off work about eight. I'll come over the instant I clock out."

It took only moments to purchase the locks she needed. Lilly was back in her car in five minutes and heading home. "Thank You, Lord, for making sure that Penny didn't witness that mess." Her daughter's feelings of security would be completely shattered if she knew what had happened at their house. Lilly wanted to get the locks installed before her daughter arrived home, but she knew it would not be possible.

Her reaction yesterday to Jon Littledeer had surprised her. Since Peter had deserted her, she'd usually been able to solve problems by herself. How quickly she'd dialed Jon Littledeer's number after discovering the break-in at her house still unsettled her. He'd proven to be an island of calm in this storm. When the twins told her his story about losing his family, her heart broke. How hard had that been? Yet despite the tragedy in his own life, he'd moved on.

There was something about the detective that touched a part of Lilly's heart that she thought long dead. She certainly was ready to rely on him. After she'd been punched this afternoon, he was the first thing she saw when she regained consciousness.

Something was going on between them. And that unsettled her as much as the mess with Peter.

Lilly pulled into the driveway and pressed the button on the garage door opener. Her heart raced as she parked the car. Everything looked normal, but at this point, that meant nothing. She gathered up the locks and walked through the door that led to the kitchen. A quick look around assured her no one had been in the house today. Quickly, she unloaded the car, carrying in Peter's things, and then read the directions on how to install the locks. The quicker she had extra security, the easier she'd rest.

She was ready to install the first lock when the doorbell rang, making her jump. She glanced at her watch. It was only seven-thirty, too early for her friend. Peering through the security peephole, she saw Jon Littledeer.

Relief flooded her heart. Jerking open the door, she fought the smile that tugging at her lips. "Detective, what are you doing here?"

"I wanted to stop by to make sure you got the locks we talked about yesterday."

She held up one of the locks. "I did."

"Good. That's what I wanted to know."

"I was about to start installing them. Would you like to supervise? My friend is on her way, but I wanted to start early."

He hesitated a moment.

"I also have to tell you about something that happened just as I was leaving Pete's place today."

Instantly, he entered the house. "What happened?"

His large size didn't intimidate her. Instead, she felt protected and at ease. It was a feeling that she'd not experienced since she was a child and her father saved her from a pack of growling dogs.

"The apartment manager came by as I was finishing up." She walked into the living room. Jon followed her. "He asked if I was done. I told him I was, but that I needed to clean the apartment. He told me not to worry about it. Then, when I mentioned the deposit, he told me not to worry about that, either. He'd just give it to me." She didn't mention she could use the money.

She went on. "He gave me the creeps. I want to search the place one more time tomorrow. I thought I might run across something that will tell me what that burglar is looking for." She tried to put the lock on the side of the window and dropped it.

Jon picked up the lock and showed her how to place it in the window track. "What did he say when you insisted you wanted to clean?" He held out his hand for the next lock. She gave it to him.

"He didn't like it. He wanted his key back right

then. I told him that Peter's rent was paid up until the end of the month."

Jon paused, his gaze locking with hers. "That wasn't wise. There's something about that guy that tells me it's not wise to cross him. You need to be careful."

He didn't need to tell her. The instant she'd exchanged words with Mark Rodgers, she'd known she should've kept quiet.

There was nothing she could say in her defense. She moved into Penny's room and handed him another lock.

He put the lock on the window. "Why don't you call me before you go to Pete's apartment tomorrow? I'll meet you there."

Her worry eased. "Thank you."

"Now, why don't you show me the locks you got for the sliding glass doors?"

The shopping bag with the locks sat on the kitchen counter. She pulled the rest of the locks out of the bag. He opened one of the packages. "Do you have a drill?"

"No."

The doorbell sounded.

Lilly glanced down at her watch. "I bet that's my friend. She probably brought her drill with her."

Jon said nothing.

When Lilly opened the door, Zoe hefted her bag of tools. "I'm here to work." Her gaze settled on Jon. "Who's the dish?" she whispered.

"He's a cop," Lilly whispered back.

Zoe paused. "Good. Then maybe you should check

out the creep in the car parked across from the house. He glared at me when I stopped in front of your house."

Jon rushed to the front door and disappeared outside. Lilly heard the squeal of tires.

Racing outside, she saw Jon on his cell phone.

"Yeah. I got the plate. It's a black Jeep Cherokee," he shouted into the mouthpiece. He rattled off the plate number to someone on the phone.

"Well, I say he's a man of action," Zoe quipped, watching from the open door.

Lilly turned to her friend. "He was here to make sure I put on the locks."

"Is this a new service the cops are providing?" Zoe asked.

Sandra Tillman, Lilly's neighbor, walked out of her house. "I got the license plate number," she yelled as she waved a piece of paper over her head. Jon moved into the street and took the paper from the older woman, who smiled and nodded.

Jon's actions and the respect he showed Sandra Tillman amazed Lilly. He came back into the house.

Zoe introduced herself. "I'm Lilly's friend, Zoe Schneider."

"I'm glad you brought a drill," Jon replied, spying the tool.

"I guess we need to fix the slider in Lilly's bedroom first," said Zoe.

Jon nodded. "You got it."

"Lilly also got a couple of dead bolts for both the front and back door."

Jon and Zoe disappeared down the hall, leaving Lilly to stare after them. They obviously didn't need her help.

She felt like she was in a nightmare she couldn't wake from. What was going on here? Why was someone after her? Did it have anything to do with Peter?

"Oh, Lord, what's going on?"

FIVE

"What did you think of Peter Burkstrom?" Jon asked Zoe as she drilled a hole in the header of the sliding glass door.

She paused and looked down over her shoulder at Jon. Perched on the step stool, she looked like a child-like woman with a deadly weapon. "You mean that weasel?"

That told him exactly what Lilly's friend thought of her ex.

She handed him the drill and motioned for him to pass her the lock. He obliged.

"Screws." She motioned with her fingers.

He complied, then changed the bit on the drill and gave it back to her. With a burst of power, the drill drove the screws into the door frame. "Pete caused Lilly no end of misery. Any man who'd desert his pregnant wife is worthless."

"From what I've heard, he eventually turned his life around."

Zoe climbed off the step stool. She slipped her drill

into her work apron. "Yeah, he did. But I wouldn't have bet on him." She picked up the remaining locks. "Let's finish the sliders in the living room." She grabbed the step stool, but he took it from her hand.

"You don't believe in redemption?" Jon asked as he followed Zoe into the living room.

She paused. "I do. But Pete was a jerk in high school. What Lilly ever saw in him is a mystery to me." She shook her head. "He left a lot of destruction in his wake. Yeah, he straightened up, but I needed to see lots of proof. Up until his death, he was good to his word."

"But you weren't going to bet on his long-term success," Jon noted.

Zoe looked down. "I'm not proud of my doubts, but I've seen more than one person claim to be one thing, then do something completely opposite."

"He was moving in the right direction, Zoe," Lilly said, walking into the hall.

Zoe looked her friend in the eye. "You're probably right, but remember, I saw the struggle you had after he left. I was the one who spent all thirty hours with you in the labor suite and in the delivery room when you had Penny. It was such a beautiful thing. How any man could miss that event is beyond me."

Lilly enfolded Zoe in her arms. "And I love you for all the support you gave me."

Jon recalled witnessing the birth of both of his girls. His precious girls. It had been one of the most moving experiences of his life.

He clamped down on the thought. He couldn't go

there. His gaze locked with Lilly's and he saw understanding and compassion in her eyes. A shared pain so intense that only God could heal it.

The doorbell chimed, breaking the tableau. Zoe walked over to the sliding glass doors in the living room. Lilly hurried to the front door. Opening it, she found Penny standing there.

Penny turned and waved to someone. "Thanks. I had a blast," she called. Walking into the living room, she took note of the visitors. "Wow. What's going on?"

"Hey, munchkin." Zoe grinned. "How are you?"

Penny ran to Zoe and gave her a hug. "What are you doing here?"

"What? I'm not welcome?" Zoe asked in mock horror.

"That's not what I meant," said Penny.

Zoe laughed and ruffled Penny's curls. "I know. I'm here to help install some locks."

Penny looked at her mother. "Mom?" she said, fear coloring her voice. Her eyes moved to Jon.

Jon stepped forward. "I told your mom that after the break-in at your dad's apartment, it would be a good idea to install extra locks on your doors and windows. And I stopped by to see if your mom got the locks. I was drafted to help Zoe put them all in."

Penny's gaze moved to her mother.

"That's all it is, sweetie. Just a precaution. After the mess in your dad's place, I realized how easy it is for someone to break in." Lilly walked over to her daughter and knelt before her. "That's all." She brushed the hair back from Penny's face.

Penny thought about it, then nodded. "I like that idea. I don't want anyone to break in our house."

Jon saw Lilly's body relax.

Penny went on. "Let me tell you about the swim this afternoon. By the way, I forgot to take my house key today. That's why I rang the bell."

Penny's chatter eased the tension in the room. As Jon worked on the doors in the living room with Zoe, he told himself that hearing Penny's chatter was a blessing. Even with the sharp pain he felt from the memory of his daughters' birth, Penny's sweet voice filled his heart with joy.

"What's this, Mom?" Penny asked. She picked up one of her father's high school yearbooks from the box by the back door.

"Your dad's things," replied Lilly.

"Why didn't you wait for me?" asked Penny, frowning.

Lilly rolled her eyes. "Someone decided to go swimming."

"You didn't tell me," Penny complained.

"The manager of the apartment complex wanted me to clean out the apartment, so I did. Pastor Kent came and picked up some things to give to families in the church."

Penny glanced at the things in the box. "Did you bring that digital picture frame?"

"I did. I tried to think of what you might like from your dad's apartment. I brought your father's yearbooks because I thought you might enjoy looking at them."

Penny took the digital frame out of the box and plugged it in. Pictures of Penny and Peter came up. Penny sat and watched pictures from the weekend they went to Taos and then she turned off the digital picture frame, her expression sad. She peered into the box from the apartment, looking through the items. Finally she pulled out a yearbook, took it to the couch and opened it.

Lilly glanced over at Jon and Zoe, who were still working to install the lock on the first sliding glass door in the living room. Earlier, when she'd heard Jon questioning her friend about Peter, she'd been mad, but she'd quickly realized that Jon was only doing his job.

Zoe's opinion of Peter didn't come as a shock, but she'd never aired it to Lilly. Zoe had endured a couple of bad relationships where the men said one thing but did another. And she'd been made a fool of in front of her friends. Those relationships had jaded Zoe, but Lilly couldn't blame her friend for her feelings. They'd spent a lot of time together while she was pregnant. Her parents were great, but Lilly had felt like such a burden to them. It was Zoe's get-up-and-do attitude that had helped Lilly through that difficult time.

Lilly had done a lot of soul-searching and had worked through a lot of self-pity, too. The Lord knew exactly who to put in her life.

"Do you need any help?" Penny asked.

Jon glanced at Penny. "I think we left the package

for this lock in your mother's room. Would you get that for us?"

"Sure." Penny raced out of the room.

Jon smiled and shook his head. When he turned back to Zoe, she was studying him. "You're a good guy."

The comment startled Lilly. Zoe didn't give men the benefit of the doubt.

"Here it is," Penny yelled and handed the package to Jon.

He glanced at the instructions and said, "You're right, Zoe. That last screw is optional."

Penny beamed. Zoe grinned. And Lilly's heart experienced a major jolt.

"Are you married?" Penny asked Jon.

Lilly's face drained of color. Before she could open her mouth, Penny continued, "Do you have any kids?"

Lilly's heart pounded in her chest. She wanted to snatch back the innocent words her daughter had spoken.

Jon turned to Penny. "I had a family, but they died."

Penny nodded. "Were they shot like my daddy?"

"No. My girls got sick and died."

Zoe stopped working and stared at Jon.

"Do you miss them?" Penny asked.

"I do." His words had been spoken so softly, but the impact nearly knocked Lilly to her knees.

"I miss my daddy," Penny confessed.

Jon nodded. "I understand."

"Will the hurt go away?"

"It will change," he answered. "Your memories of your daddy will turn from sad to happy. Your heart is sore now. Later, you heart will get better and you will remember your daddy with happy thoughts."

Penny nodded and rested her head on her arms as she sat at the dining-room table.

She watched Zoe and Jon install the last lock. "What tribe do you belong to?"

The room fell silent.

Lilly's eyes widened and her neck flooded with color. "Penny, you shouldn't—"

Jon shook his head, stopping Lilly. "I was the product of a mixed marriage. My father was Navajo and my mother was an English lady who ended up on a dig in Arizona."

Penny's eyes widened. "Really?"

Jon nodded. "Yes, they fell in love and got married."

"Wow. How cool is that?" said Penny.

He grinned at Lilly. "When I was seven, my parents, my sister and I spent a year in England. I thought I would freeze to death. Sometimes, I wouldn't see the sun in the sky for a week. I didn't like that."

"I hate it, too, when it's cloudy all day," Penny added. "Wow, if it was cloudy that long, that would be a real drag."

"It's time for bed," Lilly told her daughter.

Penny pursed her lips, but a firm look from her mother stopped the protest. "Okay." She said goodnight to Zoe and Jon, then walked down the hall and into her room.

"I'm sorry about her questions," Lilly said.

Jon smiled. "Don't worry about it. Her honesty is refreshing. Besides, Dave's girls grill me on just about everything. I discovered early on that it was best just to go with the flow."

The tension in Lilly's body seeped out.

"Well, it looks like we're all done with these locks. If there's anything you need or if you think of any new information, call me." He nodded to Zoe. "You're a handy lady with a drill."

"You ought to see me rewire a light," Zoe quipped.

Jon smiled. "I just might call you to do some rewiring for me. Last time I tried that, I saw the inside of the emergency room."

Zoe laughed.

Lilly thanked him profusely as she showed him out.

As Jon walked out the door, he heard Zoe say, "He's okay."

It looked like a party at the house. The detective was there again. Cars driving up, people coming and going. He should've threatened the woman at Peter's apartment instead of punching her out.

He'd watched as they installed the locks on the sliding glass doors. He'd have to find another way to get inside. Burkstrom could've hidden the evidence he took anywhere. He could've photographed the evidence, then destroyed it. He needed to discover what Burkstrom had done, then recover it. It was worth a lot of money to him. It was worth another man's freedom.

He thought about the garage opener that she'd used to raise the door. It wouldn't be hard to find the code.

They thought they could stop him with locks.

He smirked. They couldn't.

Jon took a gulp of his morning coffee. Setting the paper cup down on the scarred police-issue desk, he stared at his notebook as he reviewed what he knew in the Burkstrom case. From all appearances, Peter Burkstrom was killed in a random robbery. And even the break-in of his apartment could be explained. The robber had decided to see the place of the man he'd killed. He probably took Peter's wallet during the robbery. Jon could buy that, but Lilly's house being searched told him that Lilly's claim that Peter had been murdered could be true.

He typed in the license plate number that Lilly's neighbor had given him the night before.

"Mornin'," Dave greeted as he sat down. "I brought you a peanut butter cookie that the girls made last night. They thought poor Uncle Jon needed some cookies." He tossed the Ziploc sandwich bag onto Jon's desk.

Jon reached for the bag, opened it and ate the cookie in three bites. After a swig of coffee, he grinned. "Tell the girls thank-you for breakfast."

Dave nodded toward the computer screen. "What are you looking up?"

"Last night someone was watching Lilly's house. The neighbor got the license plate."

"And?"

"It comes back as a stolen plate from a vehicle owned by a little old lady in Galisteo." Jon had driven through the little town south of Santa Fe while investigating a murder last year. "She reported her plate stolen."

"So we're no closer to knowing who our perp is?"

"I'm hoping that one of those tapes we got from victim's apartment complex will show the same car that Lilly's neighbor saw last night."

"Hey, there, Mr. Littledeer," a little girl's voice said.

Jon looked up and saw Lilly and Penny standing inside the door of the squad room.

Penny waved, then held up her hands and wiggled her fingers. Lilly stood behind her daughter.

"They took my fingerprints. That ink is messy." Penny glanced down at her T-shirt. There was a small forefinger print on the hem of her shirt. She held up the fingerprint card.

Jon's gaze met Lilly's. Her lips twitched.

"So you and your mother have been fingerprinted?" Jon asked, walking toward them.

"Yes. It was way cool. When I tell my friend Tammy, she'll be jealous. She had her fingerprints taken at the mall. I got mine taken in a real police station." Penny's smile spoke of satisfaction.

"Penny," Lilly said in rebuke. "That is not very nice of you."

Penny hung her head. "Tammy is always telling me about what her daddy does at the university. How she gets to play in the president's office and do neat things. I just want her to know I do neat stuff, too."

Jon watched as the color bled from Lilly's face. He squatted down to be eye to eye with Penny. "Would you like to come and sit in a real police car?"

Penny's face lit up with wonder. "Wow! I could sit in a real police car?"

"Yes. I'll even let you turn on the lights and the siren," said Jon.

Penny turned to her mother. "Can I? Please." Lilly nodded.

"Yes."

Penny whooped her delight.

Jon grabbed Penny's hand and they left the squad room.

Lilly felt glued to the floor and she stared at the door through which Jon and Penny had disappeared.

"You've just witnessed a miracle."

Lilly turned, coming face-to-face with Jon's partner. "I don't understand."

"That's the first time I've seen Jon volunteer to entertain a little girl, with the exception of my twins." He shook his head. "It's been about three years since he lost his oldest daughter and nearly two years since he buried his younger daughter and his wife. He's good with my girls because they don't take no for an answer. And my girls know they can get to Jon. But I've seen him around other children. He holds himself away from them. His willingness to entertain your daughter is…" Dave shook his head.

The door opened and Penny stuck her head inside. "C'mon, Mom! We're waiting on you."

Dave smiled. "You better go."

Lilly felt the earth shift under her feet. Jonathan Littledeer was a force to be reckoned with.

SIX

Jon walked back into the police building. He remembered Penny's laugh of excitement when she turned on the siren on the police cruiser.

His oldest, Wendy, would've been just a year younger than Penny. Oddly, the fierce pain that usually accompanied thoughts of his daughters had changed in some way. Thoughts of his little ones still hurt, but not as much as they once had.

"Did you charm her?" Dave asked when Jon walked back to his desk.

"The car impressed her." He sat down at his desk. His gaze fell on his notebook. They needed to talk to Peter's old boss. "You want to take a little trip out to that construction company that Burkstrom worked for? See if they can tell us anything that we haven't come across?"

"Why not? And we can also stop by the lab and see if they can get anything off those tapes we got from the apartment complex."

Jon and Dave made their way to the evidence lab.

"Hey, Littledeer. You here to give me trouble?"

Johnny Longrunner asked. Johnny was a full-blooded Navajo whose great-grandfather was a code breaker during World War II.

"You get anything off those apartment tapes we dropped by?" asked Jon.

Johnny grimaced. "They are in miserable shape, Littledeer."

"You get something off them?" Dave asked.

"Of course he did," Jon answered. "He's just wanting us to know how good he is."

Johnny shrugged. "Hey, I work miracles. And those tapes needed one." Johnny accessed the scene he'd transferred from one of the tapes to his computer. "There's a shot of your victim arguing with someone outside a second-floor apartment. There wasn't a shot of his face on this footage, but—" He typed in another file name. A picture popped up in the lower corner of the computer screen. The camera aimed at the parking lot had captured a full front shot of the man who had argued with Peter. "That's your man."

The man had a beard, and the hair on his head looked black. His round face had a tough, worn quality to it, as if the man had seen his share of trouble. But it was the eyes that got Jon's attention. Soulless. Cold. Merciless.

"He's someone you don't want to meet in a dark alley," Johnny commented.

Jon had to agree with Johnny's assessment. This man would feel nothing when he killed. And if he was the man who had broken into Lilly's house, he'd have no mercy.

"Print me off the picture," Jon ordered. "We'll need it to show around."

Johnny complied.

Walking to the window, Jon stared out at the city street. They needed to find this man before another break-in resulted in Penny or Lilly getting hurt.

"I've got the picture," Dave told Jon.

"I'll send this pic to the duty captain so he can alert the patrols to be on the lookout for this man," Johnny told them.

Turning, Jon nodded and thanked him.

As Jon and Dave drove to the offices of Painted Desert Construction Associates, Dave read the file on the construction company.

"Adam Finley owns the firm. According to the bio on the firm's Web page, he worked his way up from summer jobs on construction sites to owning his own firm. His is the biggest construction company in New Mexico. The company also boasts of its work in the neighboring states of Texas, Colorado and Arizona."

"This firm, how old is it?"

"Thirty-five years old."

They pulled into the parking lot of a midrise building. In the lobby, the directory told them Painted Desert was on the seventh floor.

The instant they walked through the company's door, a young woman greeted them. "What can I do for you, gentlemen?"

Jon pulled out his badge and asked to speak to Adam Finley.

"I'll let him know you are here," said the receptionist.

At that instant, the door to an office opened and a man walked out.

"Mr. Finley, these two men are here to see you," announced the receptionist.

Adam Finley stood five-eleven and had a full head of gray hair. The weathered skin of his face spoke of his time out in the harsh sun. The man might be in his fifties, but he looked like he'd just come in from working at a job site. There was not an ounce of flab on him.

"Gentlemen, what can I do for you?"

Jon showed him his badge. "We've come to ask you about an ex-employee."

Finlay motioned them inside his office. From the window, they could see the street below and the mountains in the distance.

"Who are you interested in?"

"A man named Peter Burkstrom," said Jon.

Finley walked to his desk and leaned back against it, crossing his arms over his massive chest. "Yes. Pete worked for us. Is he in any trouble?"

"He was murdered," Jon informed him.

Finley shook his head. "I am so sorry to hear that."

Jon studied Finley carefully, watching his expression. "How well did you know him?"

"I knew him well enough to say hi at the job site, ask about the job and how it was going, but we never went beyond that. He worked with some of the foremen I know. No one said they had any problems with him."

"It surprises me," Dave interjected, "that you didn't know him very well."

Finley shrugged. "You've never worked construction, have you, detective?"

Dave shook his head.

"It's a job with a high turnover. Construction crews can have a ninety percent turnover rate from start to finish. And if it's the winter, I'll be lucky to keep those ten percent."

Jon pulled out his notebook. "When did he leave?"

Finley walked around his desk, logged onto his computer and typed in several things. "He left last May."

"Do you know why?" Jon asked.

"No. The only reason I know he quit is because Greg told me he left."

"Greg who?" Jon asked.

"Greg Majors," said Finley.

"And did Mr. Majors say why Peter Burkstrom quit?"

"Nope."

"It might help us if we talked to Mr. Majors and some of the men who worked with Peter Burkstrom," said Jon. "Also, if you could give me the names of a couple of the other foremen he worked with."

Finley nodded. "Of course. Greg is out at a work site north of the city. Let me call him and see if he's available."

Jon and Dave traded looks while Finley dialed his foreman.

"Do you want Greg to drive into the city?" Finley asked.

Jon shook his head. "No, we'll drive out to see him. That way we can talk to the men who worked with Peter Burkstrom."

Finley nodded and spoke quietly into the phone. After a minute, he hung up. "There's a bridge going up over State Highway 44 that we're working on." He gave them the mile marker where the crew was working.

"How long did Burkstrom work for you?" Jon asked.

Finley looked at his computer screen. "Off and on for five years."

"Isn't that a long time?" Jon asked.

"Yes and no. He didn't work continuously for the firm. He worked for us on several different highway sites in different states. He also worked some building jobs for the state, so I wasn't in contact with him all that time."

"Is there anything you can think of that might help us in this case? Did Burkstrom have a falling-out with someone, or did something on a job site go wrong?"

Finley rubbed his chin, glanced at the computer screen, then shook his head. "Nothing comes to mind. Like I said, no one mentioned any problems with him, and there's zero in the personnel file about problems." He rose to his feet.

Jon and Dave knew the interview was over.

At the door of his office, Finley looked at the receptionist. "Brandi, can you give the detectives a list of the men working on the bridge at Bernalillo?"

She gave Finley her pageant smile. "I'd be happy to."

"If I can be of any further assistance to you, gentlemen, please let me know." Finley shook each detective's hand, smiled and walked back into his office. The door closed behind him. However politely, they'd been dismissed.

"It will take a few moments to get the information," said the receptionist as she quickly typed into the computer and her printer sprang to life.

"How long have you worked here?" Jon asked.

"Six months," she replied.

"Does anyone from the various work sites come into town?" asked Dave.

She shook her head. "Rarely. Mr. Finley spends a lot of time visiting each project. Sometimes he meets with the suppliers here."

"It must be boring here," Dave commented.

"Usually," she said.

"Something happen recently?" Dave asked, pressing.

She pulled the paper out of the printer and handed it to Jon. "You know, Mr. Finley is very strict about the times I come in and out. If I am ten minutes late from my lunch break, he's all over my case. Well, a couple of times this last month, he's told me to go home at four-thirty. The first time, I thought he was teasing. But he wasn't." She shook her head. "The next time it happened, he gave me theater tickets for the new production of *Grease* that is playing downtown. I was out of here in less than two minutes. My boyfriend and I went that night."

The phone rang. She picked it up. "Okay, Mr. Finley." Her expression told the detectives they needed to go.

Jon pulled out his business card. "Call me if something happens or you remember anything unusual."

The detectives said nothing until they were in the car.

"What did you think?" Dave asked.

"It seems odd to me that Finley wouldn't know a man who worked for his company for five years."

"He gave us the information readily."

Jon guided the car onto the street. "Did he have a choice?"

"It is reasonable to believe Finley didn't know anything about Burkstrom but his statistics. I don't know everything about every detective on the force."

Jon shook his head. "Every man who's been with the department for more than six months you know everything about."

"That's because my wife is nosy, always asking me questions. It's easier to supply the information than to endure the endless questions."

"No, I don't buy that. We need to ask some of Burkstrom's old crew how chummy he was with Finley."

Dave laughed. "I agree. Somethin' ain't right."

"You got that itch, too?"

"Yup, my radar is yelling at me."

Lilly finished vacuuming Peter's apartment. Penny sat by the fireplace. The rest of the furniture had been removed this morning.

"Mom, I'm bored. Can we leave?"

Lilly glanced around the empty apartment. She'd checked every piece of furniture before it was removed this morning. She'd found nothing.

"Yes."

Penny whooped in delight. She ran to the door and threw it open. A startled young woman stood on the other side.

Penny stumbled back in surprise.

"I'm sorry," the woman said. "I was about to knock on the door."

"May I help you?" Lilly asked.

"I'm Julie Rose. I live here in the complex. I just wanted to tell you how sorry I am about your husband. He was a very nice man. He also was a big help to me when I moved here to Albuquerque."

"You knew my daddy?" Penny asked.

"I did," replied the woman.

Penny smiled. "Did you like him?"

"Yes. He helped bring up the furniture to my apartment and was always nice."

Penny nodded.

"Thank you," Lilly added.

The woman turned to leave, then stopped. "Do you know the names of the detectives looking into your husband's murder?"

"Yes," replied Lilly.

"Could you tell them to call me? I've remembered something else I'd like to tell them," said the woman.

"They are Detectives Jonathan Littledeer and David

Sandoval. If I see them again, I'll tell them," Lilly assured her.

The woman nodded and left.

Lilly knew she needed to call Jon.

The construction site lay north of the city, near the junction of I-25 and State Highway 44. The new bridge would replace the existing structure. A sign outside the trailer at the site proclaimed Painted Desert Construction.

Jon pulled their police-issue black sedan up to the trailer door. Before they got to the door, it opened and a young man in his early twenties barreled out, grumbling under his breath.

The door bounced off its frame.

At the same time Jon reached the steps of the trailer, another man appeared in the doorway.

"This is a closed site," the man growled.

"That may be, but I'm Detective Jonathan Littledeer and this is my partner, David Sandoval. We're here to interview Greg Majors about a Peter Burkstrom."

The barrel-chested man stepped back. "Come in. Mr. Finley told me to expect a couple of detectives from the Albuquerque PD."

Stepping into the trailer, Jon saw a desk at one end of the room, scattered with papers. Above the desk hung a detailed plan of the new bridge with the dimensions. At the other end of the trailer was a worn couch and a couple of ragged chairs.

Majors settled his bulk in the chair behind the desk. "What can I do for you, gentlemen?"

"Tell us about Peter Burkstrom," Jon answered, taking his notebook out of his shirt pocket.

"Pete worked with the company for a number of years. He worked on various projects," said Majors.

"Why'd he quit?" Dave asked.

Majors shrugged. "Can't say."

"Weren't you curious as to why someone who'd worked at your company for a long time wanted to quit?" Jon pressed.

Majors rested his hands on his knees and stared at his fingers. "I was going through a divorce. I wasn't in the mood to listen to all the men's complaints, so Pete stepped in. I guess he got tired of listening to complaints, too, because a couple of months ago, he up and quit on me."

"And you have no real idea why?" Jon pressed.

Majors shrugged. "I should, but I was too busy with my own problems, and I'm not a shrink. If he had problems, he didn't say anything to me."

Jon put his notebook back into his shirt pocket. "Do you mind if we interview some of the men?"

"No. But I'll warn you that some of the men who worked with him are no longer working on this project," replied Majors.

"Why is that?" asked Dave.

"Well, we have several projects going on in Colorado and Texas that need experienced crews to finish up on time. We have another couple of months on this bridge, so I sent some of the guys to Colorado and Texas to bring those projects in on time."

"We'll need the names of those crew members who are in different states." Jon glanced at Dave. From his partner's expression, Jon knew Dave had as many unanswered questions as he did. It seemed no one knew anything about a man who'd worked for the company for close to five years. Something was wrong. Someone was lying.

"It will take me a while to get those names together," Majors announced.

"Not to worry. We'll probably be close to an hour talking to the men here," Jon told him.

With those words, Jon and Dave left the trailer and started walking down to where the crew was working.

"How well did you know Peter Burkstrom?" Jon asked Tony Rhodes. The young man had to be in his early twenties.

"I worked with him last summer. We worked on a bridge off Highway 53 between Grants and the Zuni Indian Reservation."

The wind picked up, blowing dirt into their faces. Stepping into the shelter of the bridge abutment, Jon asked, "Did he have any problems with any of the crew?"

"Yeah, he did. He had to let go a couple of guys."

"Do you know what kind of trouble he had with them?"

Tony shook his head. "No, not really. But whatever it was, he blew up and threw the guys off the site. The project shut down for a couple of days until they were replaced."

"Do you know the names of these men?"

"Jose Heinz and Tony…uh…Ben— I don't know. Check around with some of the other guys who were at that site. They might know his name."

Jon pulled out his business card. "If you think of anything else, give me a call."

Forty minutes later, Jon discovered that only one other man there had been at that construction site the summer before. And that man added nothing to what Jon already knew.

The detectives headed back to the trailer to pick up the list of men who had worked with Peter. When Jon asked about the two men Peter had let go, Majors told them that the guys were lazy and had missed too much work. Jon asked for their addresses and got them.

As the detectives walked back to their car, Jon's cell rang.

"Littledeer."

"Jon, this is Lilly."

"Is anything wrong?" Jon asked, worried that something else might have happened at her house.

"No. When I finished cleaning Pete's apartment today—"

"You went to Pete's apartment by yourself?"

Silence greeted his question.

"Did you have any trouble with the manager?"

"No. I gave the keys back to him. I've met friendlier stray dogs than he was. I'm glad I don't have to go back there again."

He shared her sentiments. There was something about that man that didn't sit right with him.

"Uh—the reason I called was one of his neighbors, Julie Rose, came over and asked me to tell you to call her. She wants to talk to you and Dave."

He remembered the young woman. "Did she mention why she wanted to talk?"

"No. She only wanted to talk to you and Dave."

"We'll be there soon."

"Penny wants to know when you're going to come and see her garden. She has a patch that is all her own. She's very proud of her work. I think she wants to impress you with her knowledge."

Jon racked his brain, trying to determine when he could go by the church garden. "Is she there with you at the church during the day?"

"Usually. Sometimes she spends the day with my cousin Allison and her daughter. There's just so much weeding that an eight-year-old wants to do."

He laughed. "I understand. Dave's mentioned that his girls want to come by and see if real carrots grow in the ground. They have their doubts."

"Any time."

Jon hung up. Tomorrow was Dave and Marta's twelfth anniversary. He'd volunteered to take the girls to a movie in the afternoon, but they might enjoy a trip to the garden. He knew he would.

Jon and Dave pulled up to the Mission apartment complex. As they headed for the stairs, Mark Rodgers popped out of his office. "Detectives, what are you doing here?"

Jon stopped and locked gazes with the man. "We're continuing our investigation." His tone left no room for further questions.

"But the apartment is empty." Rodgers looked from one detective to the other. He opened his mouth, but Jon cut him off.

"If we need your further assistance, Mr. Rodgers, we will contact you."

He glared at the detectives, turned and walked back into his office.

"He's much too interested in this case," Dave muttered as they walked up the stairs.

"We need to run a background check on him when we get back to the station."

Dave nodded.

They walked to Julie's apartment and knocked on the door. They heard movement in the apartment; then the door opened.

"Hi," she said.

"Lilly Burkstrom called and said you wanted to talk. Have you lost my card?" Jon asked.

She shrugged her shoulders. "She was there and I— Okay, I lost your card."

The detectives moved into the apartment.

"What was it you wanted to talk to us about?"

"Well, when you asked me about Peter Burkstrom, it made me nervous. That creep who Peter argued with has been here a couple of times. I've seen him hanging around the complex. The man makes me nervous, but the more I thought about it, the more I knew I had to do the right thing. I heard part of the argument that Pete had with that guy." She moved to her couch and sat down. "Pete told the guy that he wasn't going to back down. The man stepped closer to him and said something. I didn't hear what he said, but Pete kinda went pale. The guy's been here a couple of times recently. I saw him one morning when I was late for work. Most of the people here in the complex had already gone. Me, I'd overslept. When I raced out to my car, I saw him in his car. I looked again as I drove out of the parking lot. He wasn't in his car anymore."

Dave pulled the picture from the police computer lab from his pocket and asked, "Is this the man you saw?"

She took the picture from his fingers and studied it. "That's him. When I peeked out the window, I noticed the guy had this really nasty-looking snake tattooed on his forearm." She handed the picture back to Dave.

Jon pulled out his notebook. "Can you describe the car he was driving?"

"Green. Four doors. Maybe it was an American-made car. I'm not good with cars. Ask me what kind of shoes he had on, and I could tell you."

"If you see the man again here at the complex," Jon instructed, "call 911. Don't try to confront him."

"You got it," she said.

As the detectives walked down the stairs to their car, Jon's cell phone rang.

"Littledeer," said Craig Jacobs, a fellow detective. "I've got a robbery suspect in custody that you need to talk to."

"And why is that?"

"He claims he knows who gunned down Peter Burkstrom. But he's only going to talk to the detectives on the case. He also wants to trade his information for a reduction in his charges."

"Give us ten and we'll be there."

"What is it?" Dave asked after Jon put away his phone.

"We have a jailhouse snitch who wants to trade his information for some favorable treatment."

"Let's go."

Hopefully, they would finally catch a break on this case.

SEVEN

Lilly looked down the rows of carrots. They were ready for harvesting. They'd done a once through today with the tomato plants, picking the ripe ones. Penny had had fun telling her mother which tomatoes to pick.

She walked up a row of corn plants. Penny couldn't wait for tomorrow to start picking ears of corn and pulling carrots. Her favorite part of the day was delivering the baskets to the residents of the neighborhood. She'd asked if "the detective" was coming tomorrow.

Lilly didn't understand her daughter's willingness to involve Jon in their lives. They had just buried her father. And yet, Jon seemed to respond to Penny as if they had a special connection. Jon certainly had a way with the Sandoval twins.

How had he been with his daughters?

The thing that bothered Lilly the most was that Penny wasn't the only female Burkstrom interested in the detective beyond his role of looking into Peter's death.

"You think we'll have enough volunteers tomorrow?" Pastor Kent asked, breaking into her musings.

She jumped and faced the pastor.

"Sorry. I didn't mean to startle you," he said.

"Yeah, I'm a little jumpy with all that's happened at Pete's place and at my house."

"How's Penny dealing with her dad's death?"

"I was just wondering that myself. Sometimes she's okay and other times, she cries. That I understand, but what puzzles me is that she likes the detective investigating Pete's death."

"I know you doubt it was random robbery. If you need to, you and Penny can spend some time with Rachel and me."

The son of a rancher, Kent McPhee had been raised in southern Colorado, but he'd felt a call to the ministry. He'd been at the church for a month when Lilly showed up, pregnant and in need of a job. He'd hired her with no questions asked. They'd been friends for over eight years. When Lilly's parents moved to Florida, Pastor Kent and his wife, Rachel, had become family, and they were as much a part of Lilly's life as her cousin Allison and good friend Zoe.

"I just might take you up on that offer."

He nodded. "Are we set for Saturday's harvesting?"

"We're lacking a couple of volunteers, but God is faithful, and I know we'll have enough hands."

Pastor Kent laughed. "It is good to hear my flock's faith. Sometimes God gently reminds me He is faithful. And not to doubt. Too often I feel like Peter, stepping out of that boat."

"Hey, Mom! Guess who's here?" Penny's excited

voice filled the air. She appeared around the corner with Detective Littledeer in tow. "The detective is here. He wants to talk to you." Penny skipped toward her mother. "I asked him if he's going to help us on Saturday."

Jon followed Penny down the row of corn.

Lilly smiled. "And what did he say?"

"He did that adult thing and said, 'We'll see,' but you know what that means." She rested her fists on her hips. "No."

The detective flushed. It was a rare sight. Lilly fought the grin trying to burst free. "I'm sure that if he can make it, he will. Remember, I told you about the other detective's daughters. They didn't believe me when I told them that carrots grow in the ground."

Penny giggled. "They need to come and help with the harvest. We're going to work and we'll need all the help we can get. It's on Saturday, Detective Littledeer. All the people are off on Saturday."

"Policemen work on Saturday, Penny," Lilly explained.

Penny pinned Jon with a look. "You working?"

"No," Jon confessed.

"Then you can help us?" Penny asked, pressing the matter.

Jon rubbed the back of his neck. "I'll be here."

Penny jumped up and down. "You'll bring the girls with you?"

Lilly opened her mouth, but Jon held up his hand. "I already talked with their mother. I was going to take them out to dinner and a movie while their parents celebrate their anniversary, but I think they might love a daytime excursion, too."

The smile on Penny's face wrapped itself around Lilly's heart. "We like to start early," she warned.

"What time?" asked Jon.

"Seven," Lilly replied. When he hesitated, she added, "We'll have coffee and *migas*." The rich mixture of eggs, onions, peppers and jalapeños wrapped in tortillas was a favorite here in the city.

"My wife makes the best *migas*. Once someone tries them, they volunteer to work other days just to eat them again," Pastor Kent boasted.

After a moment of hesitation, Jon said, "I'll bring the twins with me."

"Good," Penny said. "Mom told me about them, about how they didn't know about vegetables. I can show them."

"Penny, if you don't mind, I need to talk to your mom for a minute," Jon announced.

When her daughter frowned, Lilly quickly added, "Penny, why don't you go help get the boxes and baskets ready for tomorrow? Besides, you can make up boxes for the twins and Detective Littledeer."

"Okay," Penny replied.

Pastor Kent offered his hand to Penny. She took it and as they walked away, Lilly heard her daughter say, "It's probably about Dad."

Lilly's heart contracted. "Sometimes she's too smart for her own good."

Jon didn't respond to her comment, but waited until

Penny and Pastor Kent were out of earshot. "Earlier today another detective called me in to talk to a suspect. The suspect wanted to trade information for a reduced charge."

A coppery taste filled Lilly's mouth and her stomach knotted. "And?"

"It turns out that the suspect's cousin was hired by a man to kill another man. The cousin, who's just a kid, didn't ask why, but accepted the thousand dollars for the hit. The man who hired him drove him to a convenience store and pointed out the man he wanted dead."

"Pete."

"Yeah. The cousin showed the suspect a couple of the credit cards he'd pocketed during the robbery, credit cards from the guy he killed. Whoever hired him wasn't happy with his actions after the hit and the cousin disappeared."

"I knew it." Her heart pounded. "Given the break-ins it was obvious it was a murder, but hearing it makes it real." She wrapped her arms around her waist. "Did the suspect have the name of the guy who hired the kid to kill Pete?"

"No. His cousin only mentioned the name Snake."

"That's it?"

"It's more than we had before. We're looking through the gang database to see if we can come up with a Snake. It's a long shot, but we need to try everything to develop this lead."

He had a point. They had a lead and they knew for

sure that Peter's death wasn't accidental. "So where does that leave us?"

"It leaves us looking for a motive for why someone had your ex-husband killed. Can you come up with anything?"

"Maybe a couple of years ago, but Pete had straightened up."

Confused, Jon asked, "What was going on a couple of years ago?"

"Drugs, I think, I mean, I suspected. I didn't tell you earlier because I just couldn't admit to myself he was doing drugs. But Pete was very careful never to use anything illegal around Penny or me. He knew I wouldn't allow him to spend time with Penny if there was anything questionable in his life.

"When he disappeared the first time, I don't know what happened or what he did. He never told me and I never asked. When Penny was about four, Peter showed up again, got a job and wanted to spend time with his daughter. That first job with the construction firm, the job was in town. When the jobs were out of town, he'd come home on the weekends to be with Penny. The guys he worked with in construction might know more about his life."

He shook his head.

"What's wrong?"

"Finding road crews is a challenge, but we'll do it."

"Pete never was easy. A lot of fun when he was on, but if he didn't see the need to do something, he didn't." She fell silent as the bitter memories of her marriage flooded her mind.

"And what did you see in him?" Jon asked. From the slight widening of his eyes, he surprised himself with the question.

She started back toward the church and he walked alongside her. "Sometimes those wild boys have an appeal. He was wild, but he was smart. Things were easy for him. I thought he'd settle down after we married. He certainly did." She gave a snort. "He changed into someone I didn't recognize. When I got pregnant, he dropped out of school mid-semester and got a job. When he got paid on Friday, he'd stop by a bar or store and spend a good portion of the money. He'd spend the rent money or the grocery money. That led to fights. I couldn't live with that 'charm' anymore. Neither could he. He walked out one day and I didn't see him until after Penny was born. She was close to eighteen months old when he saw her for the first time."

She paused before the side door of the church. "You wouldn't have done that, would you?" The moment the words were out of her mouth, she wanted to take them back. She felt the blood rushing to her face. "I'm sorry. That was inappropriate."

A soft smile curved his lips. "I understand the frustration. I don't remember the six months after my wife's death." He looked down at the toe of his shoe. "We had just buried our daughter Rose. Roberta blamed herself for Rose's death. She went home after the funeral and took too many sleeping pills. If she could've talked to me, maybe—"

Lilly felt his pain as clearly as if it were her own. She laid her hand on his forearm. "Sometimes when you are in pain so deep, you don't think to reach out. You only think of it ending."

His gaze locked with hers.

"Did you ever consider taking Roberta's way out?" he asked.

"No, but remember I was pregnant. No matter how bleak life was, I was going to be a mother. My parents' support, Zoe's badgering and a lot of prayer were the key. And I spent a lot of time here at the church. Pastor Kent and I talked. And talked. And talked. He told me that no matter how dark the situation, if we stayed close to God, He will provide a way. He did."

Lilly remembered how the small congregation had come together to support her. One afternoon they'd surprised her with a baby shower, giving her a crib—used but newly refinished—clothes and disposable diapers. One young mother who couldn't afford any gift offered babysitting and cleaning services. They were all gifts given from the heart.

"I didn't deal well with the deaths of my family. I turned to drink to drown myself. It didn't work. Caren told me God could heal me. For her it was simple. And He did," Jon said.

"The faith of children."

"Mom, you finished yet?" Penny yelled from a door of the church.

"Yes," Lilly called. She smiled at Jon. "You remember we'll be expecting you on Saturday around seven. Bring your appetite. And the twins."

"You got it." He waved at Penny and walked to his car.

Lilly watched as he pulled out of the parking lot. What was it about the man that pulled at her senses? As she walked into the church, she remembered all the times that the Lord had provided for her while she was pregnant. If she had a need but didn't know where the help would come from, suddenly someone would come by the church with the very thing she needed.

When her parents decided to move to Florida, the Lord had placed her cousin Allison in her life. Allison, along with her daughter had provided that extra cushion of help for both Penny and Lilly. Then there was Zoe. She'd moved to Albuquerque from rural New Mexico around the same time Lilly had moved back home while she was carrying Penny, and she'd barged into Lilly's life. If it was broken, Zoe could fix it or knew whom to talk with to fix the problem. If it was a contest between Zoe and her dad as to who could fix it, Zoe always won. Lilly had her family.

Walking back inside the church, she realized again how much God had provided for her.

Jon's news about Peter's death had rattled her.

God is our refuge and strength, an ever-present help in trouble. The first line of Psalm 46 ran through her head.

He had helped her before. He would help again.

She needed to remember that verse.

"C'mon, Mom. I'm hungry and ready to go home

and eat," Penny moaned as Lilly walked into her office. Penny sat at Lilly's desk, spinning in Lilly's chair.

"Okay. Let me get my purse and then we're off." Lilly moved toward her desk, opened the bottom drawer and stared at her purse. The black purse had two zippered compartments. One of the zippers was open. She never left her purse open. "Penny, did you go in Mama's purse?"

Penny stopped spinning in the desk chair. "No."

Lilly glanced around the office. Her church directory had been moved. Several items were out of place.

A chill ran up Lilly's spine.

"Mom, what's wrong?"

The fear in her daughter's voice snapped Lilly out of her own alarm. Penny didn't need to worry.

"Nothing. Let's go home."

As she left her office, Lilly locked the door. Someone had been in her purse, but who? That scared her.

Jon pulled into the parking lot of Lilly's church at five after seven the next morning. Caren and Connie bounced around in the backseat.

"Where's the garden?" Caren asked.

"When we goin' to eat?" Connie asked. "And where's Lilly?"

Jon turned off the ignition and glanced at the girls. "Did she allow you to call her by her first name?" Jon asked Connie.

Connie hung her head. "No."

The girls slid out of the backseat. Jon took Connie's

hand. "I'm sure if you ask her, it will be okay to call her Lilly, but get permission."

Connie brightened.

They were walking toward the church when the side door opened and Lilly appeared. "Welcome. You hungry?" She directed her question to the girls.

Two heads nodded eagerly.

Penny appeared beside Lilly. The three girls stared at each other. Finally, Penny said, "Hi. My name's Penny Burkstrom. You here to help?"

The girls all started talking at the same time.

"Is it true carrots grow in the ground?" asked Connie.

Penny nodded.

"What about corn?" Caren asked.

Penny shook her head. "It grows on stalks. Taller than you...." The girls disappeared into the fellowship hall.

"I think I see the beginning of a good friendship," Lilly commented when Jon stepped to her side.

"Oh, dear. The three of them together. My mind refuses to take it in."

Lilly laughed. The sound was so pure and joyful, it went straight to his heart—the heart that he'd written off after his wife's suicide.

"Don't worry. I won't let them run over you," she assured him.

He smiled. "That's okay if they do. This is a big adventure for them. Something that they'll talk about for a long time."

As they entered the fellowship hall, the pastor

finished his prayer and everyone joined in with an amen. Jon saw that the room was filled with families. The wonderful smell of eggs, sausages and peppers filled his nostrils. A tall woman in her thirties could be seen in the kitchen, working over the stove. She called out directions to another woman, who placed a tortilla on the flat grill.

Lilly ushered Jon to the kitchen and introduced him to Rachel McPhee.

"I've heard wonderful things about your cooking," Jon said.

Rachel blushed. She took a plate with a bare tortilla on it and placed a couple of spoonfuls of eggs, potatoes, peppers and sausage on the tortilla. "I hope you enjoy."

Jon took the plate and brought it to his nose. His stomach growled. "It smells fabulous."

"Uncle Jon, where's ours?" Caren asked.

"Right here," Lilly replied, holding out two more plates.

After each person had a plate, the group settled at a table.

"How are we going to harvest?" Caren asked.

Penny launched into a speech about picking vegetables. Jon grinned as the girls planned what they were going to do.

"You better eat well, because you're going to need your energy," he said.

Lilly stared at her breakfast and Jon easily read her tension.

"What's wrong?" he asked.

Her head came up. "What makes you think anything is wrong?"

"C'mon, Lilly. Reading people is part of my job. Something is eating at you."

Picking up her paper cup filled with coffee, she took a drink. "Yesterday, after you left, I went to my office to get my purse. Someone had been in my purse."

"Why do you say that?"

"One of the compartments was open."

He frowned.

"I am very careful to close my purse. When Penny was a baby, I once left my purse open. She got into my lipstick and colored herself and the sofa, rug and anything else she could reach. When I found her, she was trying to open a pill case with aspirin. That scared me because an overdose of aspirin can kill a baby. Since that time, I am very careful to have my purse closed."

Jon's doubt disappeared. Lilly had a reason to be cautious. "Was anything taken?"

"No. Also, things in my office weren't exactly in the right place. I mean, they were not in the exact position they'd been before. I could tell someone had searched my office."

He sat back. So whoever had been looking for something in Peter's apartment had now moved on to Lilly's office. "Okay. Be sure to lock your office today. We'll see if anything is missing or out of place at the end of the day."

She nodded.

Pastor Kent stood and welcomed all the volunteers.

"Once you finish your breakfast, please move out to the garden. We'll split you into teams and assign you different parts of the garden. You'll get a cardboard box or a large basket for the vegetables. And before we start, I want to thank everyone for their help. God has blessed this ministry far beyond anything that I expected. I had the idea. Lilly put the legs to the garden. Lilly, please stand."

Lilly got to her feet. Applause greeted her. She waved it off and sat back down. Jon glanced at Penny. She beamed with pride for her mother. The twins studied Lilly, whispered to each other, then nodded. He had a feeling they were plotting something.

"Swallow that last bite and let's start harvesting," Pastor Kent encouraged.

Lilly stood again. "One last thing. When you have a full box or basket, set it aside so our runners can bring it back to the fellowship hall. They will also bring you an empty box or basket."

"Any other instructions?" Pastor Kent asked.

"Have fun." Lilly sank back down.

Jon leaned over and whispered, "Is your office locked?"

"No. I opened it to put my purse in my desk," Lilly replied.

"Do that now. I'll manage the girls and meet you outside."

She nodded.

He watched as she left the hall.

"You like her, don't you, Uncle Jon?" Caren asked.

Her sister sat beside her. Penny stood at the garbage can between tables.

He looked down at Caren. "Of course I like her. She's a nice lady."

Caren crossed her arms and pursed her lips. "I mean, you like her like Daddy likes Mom."

Shock raced through him. "What?" he sputtered.

"He does," Connie agreed, her voice filled with certainty.

He wanted to protest, but Penny had rejoined them.

"Let's go and I'll show you how to pull carrots," Penny declared.

The twins gave him a smug grin.

"Let's go discover where carrots really come from," Caren commented.

The twins turned and followed Penny out of the hall. Jon trailed after them, wondering how he'd managed to come out on the losing end of that conversation.

What really worried him was that Caren had read the expression on his face. What were his feelings for Lilly Burkstrom?

Lilly locked her office. She'd hid her purse in a different place, behind the seed catalogs she kept on a corner bookcase. She hurried outside and saw Penny, Caren and Connie setting a box beside a row of carrots.

"Just grab it here," Penny instructed, her hand around the leaves of a carrot near the ground, "and pull." She demonstrated. The carrot popped out and she held it up as if it were a victory prize.

The twins' eyes grew large. Penny brushed the dirt off the carrot.

"Let me see," Caren demanded. Penny handed her the carrot. The twins inspected it. "It's a real live carrot."

"Sure. Bite into it," said Penny.

"Ick," Connie muttered. "It's dirty."

Penny nodded toward a bucket of water by the church. "Go wash it off and see."

Connie took the carrot, walked to the bucket and swished the carrot around in the water. When it was clean, she took a bite. She carefully chewed. After a moment, she swallowed. "It's a carrot."

Penny nodded. "I told ya."

Caren moved to the next plant, grabbed the leaves and pulled. "Look!" She held up her prize.

"Let me," Connie cried, moving to the next plant. She popped the carrot out of the soil. The expression on her face made Lilly smile.

"I was right," Penny noted.

Jon shook his head and grinned. His expression was filled with love, joy and a tinge of regret. He had to be remembering his girls. Lilly wanted to walk over to him and hug him.

The thought startled her. He turned, and his gaze locked with hers. She felt the electricity pass between them. Something had blossomed between them that neither of them had anticipated.

The question was, did she want to pursue it? Did he?

The three girls worked their way down the row, pulling out carrots. Jon trailed along behind them.

Connie grabbed Jon's hand. "Try it, Uncle Jon."

He laughed and pulled the next carrot. "I've got one." Holding up his prize, he grinned at the girls. They giggled.

Lilly turned away to check on the rest of her volunteers.

The sounds of laughter and happy chatter filled the air. One team of volunteers worked on the rows of spinach and green peppers. Another team worked close to the church, where the tomato plants were staked. Another team had disappeared among the rows of tall corn. Lilly checked the team working on the tomato vines.

"Allison, you need another basket?" Lilly asked. Her cousin had shown up this morning. Allison's daughter, Nancy, was working with her mother.

"What's Penny doing?" Nancy asked.

"She's showing a couple of new girls how to harvest carrots," said Lilly.

Nancy looked at her mom. "Can I help Penny? I mean, Penny and I did this last year. She might need some help."

Allison laughed. "Go."

Nancy disappeared around the corner of the church. Allison turned to Lilly. "Since I've lost my helper, I'll need another basket."

As Lilly started back to the fellowship hall to get a basket for Allison, she wondered how Jon would handle another eager girl. She needed to check on them.

The stacks of empty cardboard boxes and baskets

sat inside the door of the fellowship hall. She put the boxes outside the door, then lifted off the top basket and carried it back to Allison.

"I'll check on our daughters after I put this batch of tomatoes in the fellowship hall," Lilly announced. She traded the empty basket for a full one and headed back to the hall.

Lilly put the basket of tomatoes on the table inside the fellowship hall. At the door, a man appeared. He was dressed in jeans and a plaid shirt, which was open to reveal a white T-shirt underneath.

"Here you are," he said. He handed her a box filled with ears of corn. She took the box and placed it on the table. When she turned back, he was still standing there, staring at her.

Her stomach clenched.

She tried to smile, but his stone-faced expression didn't invite it. "Do you need another box? Because I left them outside the door."

He studied her for a moment more. He wore his hair in a ponytail and he looked like he hadn't shaved in several days.

On his forearm, under the partially rolled-up sleeve, she spotted a tattoo of a snake. A snake curled and ready to strike. When her gaze met his, she felt a chill run down her spine.

Jon's words rang in Lilly's head. The guy who hired the kid to kill Pete was named Snake.

She fought her terror.

"No, I don't need another box. There are plenty out

there. I just wanted to bring that full one to you." His gaze bore into hers.

She read clearly that he'd left something unsaid. He was here to send her a message.

But what?

Just when she thought she might have to run into the church proper to get away, he turned and walked out the door. He disappeared down a row of cornstalks.

The instant she could no longer see him, she raced out into the garden, to where Jon was working with the girls. Several people called to her, but she ignored them and headed straight to Jon.

The girls shouted a number each time they pulled a carrot.

"Ten," yelled Penny.

"Eleven," called Connie.

Even Nancy had joined the game. "Seven, eight." She waved her two prizes.

"C'mon, Uncle Jon. You're falling behind," said Caren.

"Who said you could beat me?" Jon grinned, but when he saw Lilly, his smile disappeared. He met her halfway up the row of carrots.

His hand captured her upper arm. "What's wrong?"

"A guy just handed me a box full of corn. He had a snake tattooed on his forearm. There was something in his eyes—"

He didn't doubt or question. "Which way did he go?"

"Down a row of corn."

"Stay with the girls," he shouted as he raced away.

The girls paused. "Where's Uncle Jon going?" Caren asked.

Lilly forced a smile. "He's going to check on something for me. I'm going to stay with you guys until he gets back."

The explanation satisfied the girls, and they went back to work on the row of carrots.

Fear clawed the inside of her chest. The look in that man's eyes had been pure evil and Jon was racing toward it.

"Lord, please keep him safe," Lilly whispered.

EIGHT

Jon ran toward the tall rows of corn. When he turned up one of the rows, he saw a woman and two little girls picking the ears of corn. "Did anyone come down this row in the last five minutes?" he asked as he walked toward them.

The woman smiled. "The helper who collected our boxes. He picked up our full box and took it to the fellowship hall. He brought back an empty box."

"Which way did he go?" asked Jon.

The woman shrugged. One of the little girls pointed toward the church. "I saw him walking that way."

Racing off, Jon wondered what this suspicious character wanted from Lilly. When he charged into the fellowship hall, several people were there, dropping off baskets.

"Anyone come through and head into another part of the church?" Jon asked a man and two teens.

"No, we've haven't seen anyone," the older man replied.

"How long have you been in here?" Jon quizzed.

"We just came in," one of the teens answered.

Jon nodded and walked down the hall to the church offices. He checked the door to Lilly's office. Locked.

He tested all the other doors. All were locked.

Jon walked out the front door and scanned the parking lot. Nothing moved. He could hear the joyful voices of those harvesting the vegetables.

He debated about calling Dave with the news. Marta wouldn't mind, but at this point, there was nothing Dave could do. He'd wait until tomorrow.

As Jon walked through the garden, he questioned the volunteers, if anyone had seen a man with a tattoo of a snake on his arm. No one had seen him.

He worked his way back to where the girls and Lilly stood.

"You didn't find him," Lilly remarked.

"No, but a few volunteers working on the corn said he gathered up their box. But other than that, no one has seen him."

"The offices?" Lilly asked.

"Everything's locked up tight."

Lilly took a deep breath. "I've got work to do."

He opened his mouth to protest.

"Jon. I will *not* cower. People depend on these vegetables."

"Can someone else do it?"

"No."

He didn't like this. Looking around at the girls, he realized that they had observed the back-and-forth between them. "Girls, we're going to help Penny's mom." He paused and made sure he had Lilly's attention. "What's next?"

Lilly pursed her lips and he thought she was going to refuse their help. "Let's go back to the fellowship hall. I have a sign I want to put out."

"Ah, Mom, I don't want to be stuck inside," Penny grumbled.

Nancy didn't look any happier about being stuck inside. "Could we go back and help my mother?"

"That sounds like a good idea," Jon replied.

"Uncle Jon," Caren whined. "I don't want to stop. Can we go with them?"

Jon knew he couldn't leave the girls alone, but he didn't want Lilly to be alone. "Well, I have a better idea."

Lilly's eyes widened.

"I'm going to call another couple of volunteers to help," he whispered in Lilly's ear. "They're cops." He pulled out his cell phone and phoned Dave. If this guy showed up again, they'd nab him.

Dave soon showed up with Marta. As they approached the girls, one of the twins spotted her parents. "Mom, what are you doing here? I thought you and Daddy were smooching," Connie announced.

Marta flushed but quickly recovered. "Well, your dad and I heard how much fun you two were having, so we wanted to come and share it with you."

Lilly glanced at Jon, then turned back to Dave and Marta. "You're welcome to help. We need all the assistance we can get."

"It sounds exciting," Dave replied.

Within minutes, Pastor Kent met the newcomers and they were put to work.

Jon and Dave gathered the girls together.

"Now, Mom and I don't know anything, so don't leave us by ourselves or Mom might panic," Dave confessed.

Dave's comment earned him a glare from Marta. But Connie took her mother's hand and Caren took her father's hand. "We'll show you," Connie assured them.

Dave motioned to Penny and Nancy. "Why don't you come with us, since you two are the experts in this?"

Turning to her mother, Penny asked, "Is that okay, Mom?"

"Yes." Lilly squatted and smiled at her daughter. "I know you'll do a great job. Check with the team harvesting the green beans. When you can't find anything else that needs picking, take everyone to the fellowship hall. We'll start to set up the assembly lines for the boxes and baskets."

"Okay." Penny turned and led her little team across the garden.

"I'm sorry that your partner had to come," Lilly said to Jon, watching her daughter. Penny chatted all the way across the garden, giving the others a running commentary about what they were seeing.

"Don't worry about it. This is not the first time that Dave and Marta have spent their anniversary on the job." Jon smiled. "This is a high point for Marta. There was the anniversary before the twins were born when we had to investigate a murder and ended up at the city dump. Marta sat in the front seat of our car while Dave and I sifted through trash. Then later they went to a taco stand for their anniversary meal. Of course, the romance was minimized because I was hungry, too, and ate with them. I brought my wife home tacos that night."

His story reminded Lilly of Jon's loss.

"I've got a couple of other men coming. They're off-duty patrolmen. We'll let them know what we're looking for," Jon said.

The rest of the morning passed without anyone spotting the man with the snake tattoo on his arm. Penny directed her little band working through the green peppers, green beans and eggplants. Two off-duty officers showed up around ten o'clock. Jon huddled with them.

When he rejoined Lilly, she asked, "What did you tell them?"

"Told them who we were looking for. They'll mingle with different teams."

Lilly's tension eased. Surely with all the police they had helping them, they could find the man with the tattoo if he was still there.

Jon helped Lilly take in boxes and basketfuls of vegetables and organize them on the long tables in the fellowship hall. By eleven, the garden had been harvested. The volunteers gathered in the hall. After a lunch of tacos and burritos prepared by Rachel McPhee, the assembly lines fell into place.

Lilly stood on a bench. "Now, we're going to assemble our boxes and baskets. Each table should have piles of each vegetable we harvested. Take a box or basket from the end of your table and put several ears of corn, tomatoes and whatever else we have in it. When we're finished, I'll pass out the names and addresses of the families who will get these boxes and baskets. When you're ready, go."

A cheer went up. Happy voices filled the room as people put together the boxes and baskets.

Jon and Lilly worked together on one of the assembly lines, putting vegetables in the boxes and baskets.

"This is quite a production," Jon said, observing the room full of people. He felt better with Dave and the two patrolmen here, but he was still worried. If this latest guy with the snake tattoo was the same one who'd hired the kid to kill Pete, he wouldn't hesitate to kill again. They'd talked to the missing kid's mom, who admitted she knew her son had done something he shouldn't have done. She feared she'd never see him again. She was probably right. This killer wasn't going to leave anyone to ID him. Which was why he worried over Lilly's encounter with the killer.

"Jon?" Lilly touched his arm.

Her touch brought him out of his worries. "I'm sorry. What did you say?"

From the look in her eyes, she understood his worry.

"I was telling you about how the harvest began. It's grown a bit since Pastor Kent and I put together baskets of tomatoes, chilies and corn that first time. I think we gave away eight baskets."

"How'd you come up with the idea?"

"Pastor Kent and I were throwing around ideas on how to reach the neighborhood. His mother had a garden on their ranch, which the children of the ranch hands enjoyed helping with. He thought it might bridge the gap with the poor in the neighborhood. He was right. We were standing in the garden late in the season when one of the neighborhood kids wandered in. He saw the green tomatoes on the vine. He didn't know what they were. When I told him they were tomatoes, he didn't believe me. He told me tomatoes were red and were sold at the store. I told him to come back in a few days and see if the tomatoes had changed color.

"He did. The next day he brought a friend. They were would-be gang members. I gave them tomatoes to take home. He kept coming by and asking questions.

"When it was time to harvest, I asked him to come by and help and I told him that he could take home some of the vegetables. He showed up with two friends and helped. They took a basketful of vegetables home that day. His mother came to the church the next day and told us that we'd saved her son.

"When we started planting the garden the next spring, my guy showed up. He had his mother and several other people with him. That young man is now working with the Department of Agriculture here in New Mexico."

Lilly beamed. "Of course, there was a lot of prayer that occurred in that garden. Pastor Kent said he sometimes felt like Adam in the Garden of Eden, finding new things the Lord wanted him to do."

Jon and Lilly reached for the ear of corn nearest them at the same time. His hand settled over hers. Her gaze flew to his. He didn't move his hand.

"You're amazing," he whispered.

She opened her mouth to respond, then closed it and shook her head. "I'm no hero. This is Pastor Kent's idea. At the time I was feeling sorry for myself, complaining to God. My husband had left me and I was pregnant. I found myself outside the church, looking at an empty lot filled with weeds and rocks. I doubted Pastor Kent's vision. How was a garden going to help? What good would tomatoes do? My vision was too small."

He squeezed her hand. "But you trusted in God."

He saw tears gather in her eyes. What had he said that made her want to cry? He pulled his hand away.

"Thank you."

He was totally lost. "For?"

"Reminding me that God sees the whole picture. When we started growing vegetables that first year, I had no idea what would blossom here. But He knew."

"And you trusted."

She nodded. She put the last ear of corn in the box in front of them. He added the last of the carrots. The box moved down the table and the others finished loading it with vegetables.

Looking around, Lilly saw that most of the tables had finished packing their boxes and baskets.

"I need to get the address lists and start handing them out." She walked toward her office. Jon followed.

After unlocking her office, she grabbed the lists from her desk.

"Everything look okay?" Jon asked.

Dave appeared in the doorway. "Anything wrong?"

"No," Lilly answered. "I just needed to get the address lists."

She locked the office door and they headed back to the fellowship hall. Lilly handed the volunteer drivers their address lists so that they could deliver the vegetables to the families.

Pastor Kent waved everyone into silence. "Thank you for your help. As you have given of yourselves this day, the Lord knows your work. Lord, we pray that these gifts will be received with open hearts, and bless those who worked and who'll receive."

"Amen," came the response.

The drivers headed for their cars. The boxes and baskets were loaded up. Lilly gave Allison and Nancy a hug and thanked them for their hard work. Lilly had her list of recipients. The twins, Penny, Jon, Dave and Marta followed Lilly to her car.

"I want to go with Penny's mom to help with the deliveries," Caren announced to everyone. "We've worked all day and I want to help give the vegetables to the people."

"Me, too," Connie chimed in. "It's not fair not to get to see them."

Penny joined the fray. "They're right, Mom."

Dave looked at his wife.

Jon stepped to his partner's side. "Why don't you

guys go out to dinner? I'll keep the girls. We'll go out to eat." He looked at Lilly. "That is, after we finish delivering our boxes of vegetables."

The girls yelled their agreement.

Dave didn't hesitate. "Ladies, I expect you to be on your best behavior for Uncle Jon."

Caren nodded her head. Connie's mouth curved into a wide smile.

Jon saw the two patrolmen walk into the parking lot. He motioned them over. Lilly hung back while he questioned the men. Their suspect had not been spotted this afternoon. As they wrapped up the conversation, Lilly stepped forward and thanked both men.

He turned back to Lilly and the girls. "I don't think we'll all fit into one car. Why don't you put some of the baskets and boxes in my car, and we'll caravan together?" He wasn't going to allow Lilly out of his sight with their killer stalking her. Lilly understood his caution and didn't argue.

For the next two hours they delivered vegetables.

His little tête-à-tête with Lilly had had the exact result he wanted. He'd scared her. He hadn't found it yet. Burkstrom had hidden the evidence well. He hadn't run across it in his search of the man's apartment, which meant the ex had it.

He didn't think Burkstrom had a safety-deposit box, so he knew that the ex had to have it.

She might need another push in the right direction.

That could be arranged.

He watched in satisfaction as the last car left the parking lot. His boss was getting antsy.

He found he was enjoying this little game of cat and mouse. This time the hunt had entailed more than just pulling the trigger.

His next move would be to catch her alone and ask where the information was hidden. If she didn't cooperate, he'd have to use more persuasive measures. His boss was demanding the proof and he didn't like demanding bosses.

NINE

After dinner, the girls all climbed in Jon's car to ride to Lilly's, since she'd invited them to share the chocolate cake she'd baked.

It took less than five minutes to get to her house. Lilly punched the button on the garage door opener. She felt a moment of panic when she looked into the garage and saw that her garbage cans were in the wrong place.

After turning off the ignition, she got out of her car and dashed to the driver's door of Jon's car. She motioned for him to roll down his window.

"The trash cans have been moved," she whispered.

He didn't comment, but simply turned to the girls. "Stay in the car for a minute."

Penny started to protest, but Caren sighed and sat back in her seat. "It's a cop thing. Sometimes my dad checks the house before we go in."

"Really?" Penny asked, her eyes wide with incredulity.

"Yeah. Sometimes Dad gets really weird. You just ignore it," advised Caren.

"Oh." Penny crossed her arms and settled beside the twins.

Jon reappeared several minutes later. He nodded.

"See? What did I tell you?" Caren calmly said. "Everything's okay." She sighed. "We're used to this. Dad does strange stuff. Isn't that so?" she asked her sister.

"Yes. And some of the things Uncle Jon does are just as strange," said Connie.

"Oh." Penny didn't question or comment, but simply accepted Caren's explanation.

The girls scrambled out of the backseat and walked into the garage. Lilly walked to the back door. Jon stood inside the kitchen door.

"How is everything?" Lilly whispered when she reached the kitchen.

"If someone's been in here, I can't tell. It's okay now," he reported.

Lilly collapsed into one of the kitchen chairs. Her mind registered the girls giggling in the other room. Lilly looked up at Jon. "What does Peter's murderer want?"

"I wish I could tell you. I've called other police departments to have their detectives interview the other men who were on your ex-husband's construction crew. We have a couple of names of disgruntled ex-workers and we are checking them out. We're also trying to ID the man with the snake tattooed on his arm. And we don't know if it's the same guy who kept coming around the armor car company that Peter worked for."

Lilly ran her fingers through her chin-length hair. "I wish I knew what this was about. I never really wanted to know about Pete's life after our divorce. It seemed safe not to know."

Jon caught her hand in his. "Don't."

The warmth and strength in his hand eased her fear. "Don't what?"

"Don't blame yourself for things you can't control." He stared at her hand, running his thumb over her knuckles. He looked up. "I've walked that road. I blamed myself for carrying the defective gene that brought that terrible disease into my daughters' lives. If I hadn't had that gene...if Roberta hadn't had it, too..." He remained silent for a long time, then whispered, "In my distress I called upon the Lord, and cried to my God for help."

She recognized the psalm.

"Psalm 18:6. It helps when I start looking at things the wrong way. You are trying to control things that you have no control over. It took a long time for me to learn that lesson. More than once in my prayers, I blamed myself. You need to remember you didn't control your ex. It would help if we knew what this person is looking for. But it is not your fault," Jon said.

Her eyes filled with tears. His words resonated within her heart. She was trying to blame herself for things beyond her control. "What breaks my heart is Pete had just started turning things around. Penny finally had a dad."

Jon still had his hand around hers. He brought her

hand to his lips and kissed the palm. "Penny has a wonderful mom."

"Hey, Mom, where's that digital picture frame with all the pictures in it?" Penny yelled.

Jon released her hand and Lilly felt the loss in a way that she didn't want to admit. "It's in the living room. The flash drive is in the drawer of the end table it's on."

"Okay," called Penny.

"We want to see the water park where Penny went with her father this summer," Connie explained.

"We're trying to convince Dad to take us there," Caren added.

"And Mom, can you cut the cake?" Penny threw over her shoulder as she walked into the living room.

Jon shook his head. "There's more to their desire to see the pictures than just seeing Penny's fun times." Rubbing his neck, he added, "I think I might be in trouble with my partner."

"Then you'll have to be the one who takes them to the water park." Lilly laughed at Jon's expression. She got up, then gathered plates, glasses, forks, a knife and the cake.

They heard the "wows" and "neats" coming from the living room as Penny gave commentary on each picture in the frame.

"What is that?" Caren asked.

Penny shrugged. "I don't know. Mom. Mom."

Jon and Lilly walked into the living room. The girls were gathered around the digital picture frame, which sat on an end table. What was on the screen wasn't a picture. A moment later the image changed to some sort of typed page.

"Mom," Penny cried. "What's going on?"

Lilly approached the end table. She felt Jon behind her.

The image changed again, to what appeared to be some sort of invoice. The invoice was for concrete. It dissolved and another one appeared. This one was for rebar.

"Mom, what happened to my pictures of the water park?" Penny asked.

The image changed again. A shot of the water park, with Penny going down the water slide, filled the frame.

"There it is. It's so neat," Penny told the girls.

The next image was another of the concrete invoice.

"What's going on?" Penny asked again.

Lilly glanced at Jon. "I think maybe your dad added some things to the pics."

"Why do I want to see that? Why'd he do that?" Penny asked.

Those were good questions. "Why don't you show the girls the album from the time we went to Disney World and you visited Grandma and Grandpa?" said Lilly. "I'll go and cut the cake."

Penny considered the suggestion. "Okay. That's better than those stupid old pictures."

The girls went back to Penny's room. The digital frame continued to cycle through the pictures. Lilly watched with incredulity as the shots of the invoices reappeared on the screen. "Do you think this is what that man is after?"

"I don't know, but let me take that flash drive and have the guys in the evidence lab analyze the invoices. What the invoices mean, I don't know."

Lilly turned off the frame and pulled out the flash drive. Jon slipped the small drive into his pocket.

Lilly headed to the kitchen. "Let's go get cake."

Lilly quickly placed slices of cake on individual plates and poured glasses of milk. After they enjoyed the cake, Connie yawned and put her head on the table.

Jon glanced at his watch. Eight forty-five. "I don't know about the twins, but this detective has put in a long day. Caren, Connie, let's go."

The girls put up a token protest, but their tiredness showed in the slump of their shoulders.

Penny stepped to her mother's side and waved goodbye to Jon and the twins as they climbed in Jon's car. "I wish I had a sister."

The statement startled Lilly. Her mind went blank.

"It would be neat to be a twin," Penny said wistfully.

Relief swept through Lilly. Maybe her daughter didn't mean that she wanted a sibling. "It is a special bond." Lilly bent down and looked her daughter in the eyes. "But you are so special that two of you would've knocked me flat. I don't think there could be another little girl as precious, smart and pretty as you."

Penny smiled. "Thanks, Mom."

Later, as Lilly lay in bed, trying to sleep, her mind raced from image to image. The day spent with Jon, Penny and the twins had been a joy. More than once, he'd had to help the girls with the harvesting. He'd laughed when Caren had managed to pull up a bunch of carrots and got dirt in her mouth. Caren was very fretful about getting dirty. She'd enjoyed picking the vegetables, but getting dirt in her mouth had been a major setback. Jon had run to the metal tub filled with bottles of water that had been set between the rows, had grabbed a bottle of water and given it to Caren. It had taken the entire bottle for Caren to feel that she'd live. Jon hadn't scolded her, but had simply helped.

He'd also taken direction well. Penny could be a little dictator when she wanted to be. She'd repeatedly instructed them on how to harvest the different vegetables until Connie had challenged her. Somehow Jon had soothed everyone's feathers.

He would've made a wonderful father. Patient, loving and handsome—

Lilly stopped herself. Handsome had nothing to do with fatherhood. Peter had had his share of good looks and yet he hadn't been the model parent.

Jon's words to her tonight about being responsible for Peter's shortcomings hit home. She'd blamed herself for Peter's unhappiness and desertion. Maybe if she'd been a better wife or better cook, or if she'd understood him more…

Jon's words rang through her brain. She wasn't responsible for things she couldn't control. Peter's reactions she couldn't control, just as Jon couldn't control what genes he'd inherited. It made sense when she applied that logic to Jon's situation. She now saw it made sense when she applied it to her own.

"Thank You, Lord, for letting me see that."

When she turned over in bed, she wondered why Peter had put those invoices in with the pictures of himself and Penny on the digital frame. What did those invoices contain that Peter would put them on the flash drive for the digital frame? It made no sense. But none of this made any sense.

Jon carried a sleeping Caren to the front door. Marta opened the screen door and pointed the way to her daughter's bedroom. Dave soon followed with the other twin. He placed his daughter on the bed. Marta took over, helping the girls change into their nightgowns.

Jon walked to the kitchen. Dave joined him.

"You want some coffee?" Dave asked.

Jon shook his head. "I hope you and Marta had a nice dinner."

"We did, but that's not why you're staying."

Jon rubbed the back of his neck. "Before dessert at Lilly's house, the girls wanted to see some pictures of Penny and her dad. When they turned on this digital frame that had belonged to Peter Burkstrom, they saw more than pictures. Apparently, our victim had put pictures of some invoices on the frame's flash drive."

"What kind of invoices?" Dave asked.

"For concrete and rebar. My guess is that they have to do with some building project he'd worked on." He reached into his pocket and brought out the flash drive. "I have the drive. I thought I'd drop it off with our tech people to see if they can provide some insight.

If they come up with nothing, they can send the information to the state lab. Maybe they can pinpoint which construction project these materials were purchased for."

"Sounds like a plan." Dave leaned back against the countertop and folded his arms over his chest. "How was your dinner?"

The tone Dave used set him on edge. "The girls insisted on Penny and Lilly joining us. They've found a friend in Penny. Penny feels the same way about them."

Dave nodded. "Are the girls the only ones with feelings?"

Jon didn't have to ask what his partner meant. He knew. "You know we don't involve ourselves with family members of the victim."

"Really?" Dave shook his head. "You could've fooled me."

Jon glared at him.

"When have the rules stopped you, Jon?"

Who was he kidding? His partner knew him. The reason Dave and Jon worked so well together was that they thought alike. If it hadn't been for Dave and Marta, he never would've recovered from the deaths of his wife and children. But they'd cared for him and prayed for him. They'd thrown out a lifeline and he'd grabbed it. "I'm not ready, Dave."

Dave pushed away from the counter and rested his hand on Jon's shoulder. "I think you are. There's a spark in your eyes when you're with Lilly and Penny. And Penny is taken by you. You don't have to rush anything, friend. Just open your heart. Everything else will just happen."

"What I need to do is find out why someone is after them, and the best way to protect them is to find out who killed Lilly's ex."

"That's true." Dave didn't push, but in his eyes, Jon saw his encouragement.

"G'night."

"Remember what I said," Dave called out.

Jon walked through the living room and out the front door.

"What is he supposed to remember?" Marta asked, joining Dave in the kitchen.

"I think my partner's heart has come back to life again. I told him to listen to it and give it a chance."

"Amen."

The instant Jon entered the police building, he walked down to the evidence lab. He'd called Johnny this morning and asked him to meet him at the police station. He knew his friend would come in on Sunday.

"Littledeer, you look like you've just come off a twenty-four-hour stakeout. What have you been doing?" Johnny Longrunner asked.

What he'd done all night was wrestle with the words his partner had spoken. Was what was in his heart so obvious?

Jon held up the flash drive. "I called you because I need your expertise. I didn't want a comment on my appearance."

"You look like something my cat would drag in."

Jon tried to glare, but his head hurt too much. "I need for you to pull up the invoices on this drive and see if you can tell me exactly what they're for."

Johnny waved his hand. "Give it."

Jon gave him the drive.

It only took seconds for the pictures to come up on the screen.

"A trip to a water park?" Johnny commented.

Jon didn't bother with a reply.

The invoices came up. Johnny stopped the progress of the images. "Oh, looks like someone took pictures of these invoices and wanted to hide them."

"I think so, too. This flash drive is from my murder victim. He obviously mixed these pictures of invoices in with pics of his daughter in order to hide them. But why? What are they for? Look at the next picture," Jon commanded.

Johnny clicked the forward button.

The invoice for rebar came up.

"Well, this is for building something, such as a road. Or a swimming pool. We'd need to call the company and ask what the rebar was used for."

"You want to give me a guess?" Jon asked, pressing. "Would a highway go with the companies who wrote these invoices?"

"Yes. The best thing to do is to call the companies tomorrow."

Jon ran his fingers through his hair. "Give me back the flash drive."

"Sorry I can't be any more helpful than that. Tomorrow, call the companies and ask." Johnny ejected the drive and gave it back to Jon. "What's got you tied up in knots?"

"It's this case. Something going on that's below the surface. What it is— Well, I think those invoices might hold the key. It's been that way from the moment I told the victim's ex-wife."

"Send your invoices to Sam Maxwell. He works wonders with evidence."

"Thanks for coming in, Longrunner."

Jon left the evidence lab, walked to his desk and put the flash drive in the middle drawer. He must look bad if Johnny was on his case. He'd struggled with a lot of things last night.

There was nothing like your partner telling you that you were eyeballing a woman with hunger in your eyes. He wanted to tell Dave he was nuts, but he couldn't lie to Dave. Jon's heart had suddenly started to beat again.

Lilly.

He rolled her name around his brain. Her beauty equaled that of the flower for which she'd been named. He found himself making up reasons why he needed to see her, talk to her. And Penny. No one would ever replace his girls, but Penny touched a part of his heart that could still love.

Precocious and smart. Of course, keeping up with girls was challenging, but Penny took it to an entirely new level. She certainly knew how to give directions. She'd told each of them how to harvest.

So what was he going to do?

And what was the meaning of the invoices?

He sat down, then logged into the police network. Removing his notebook from his sports-coat pocket, he typed in the names of the two men that had had a beef with Peter because he'd tossed them off a construction site. Jose Heinz and Ben Mentor. Ben Mentor was the name of the second man Peter had fired.

He got hits on both. Mentor had been convicted of selling false IDs and was now in the Colorado State Penitentiary at Cañyon City. Hernandez also had a record: he had spent time in a New Mexico state prison and had been released three months ago. Jon read through Hernandez's physical description. He had a snake tattoo on his right forearm.

Jon printed out the booking photo of Hernandez. Was this the guy who'd been threatening Lilly?

Glancing at his watch, he realized it was nine-thirty. He needed to hurry—he had only fifteen minutes to make it to the church. If he was late, the twins would be all over his case.

Lilly joined the congregation with the last chorus of "Amazing Grace." She glanced around the church and saw the faces of many of the volunteers who had harvested vegetables yesterday. There were several new faces in the crowd. Her gaze caught sight of Diego Ibarra, her first success story connected to the garden. He smiled and nodded at her. The instant the last note of the hymn died, Lilly made her way down the center aisle.

"What are you doing here?" Lilly asked, hugging Diego.

"I heard you had your big vegetable harvest yesterday. Mom called me and told me about what a success it was." Diego had turned into a tall young man with brown eyes that sparkled. There was a young woman by his side.

"Who's this?" Lilly asked.

"This is Tina Moore. She works with me at the state office."

Lilly shook Tina's hand. From the looks the two traded, Lilly didn't doubt that Diego had brought her home to meet his mother.

"Where's Penny?" he asked.

"She's helping in the children's church. I'll get her. You stay here. I know she'll be excited to see you."

Lilly hurried down the hall to the room where the children's service was held. Suddenly, a man stepped out of the side hall and ran into her. His hand caught her arm.

Lilly gasped. "I'm so—"

The man with the snake on his arm. He lowered his head and whispered, "I need what your ex stole. You have it. I'll make arrangements with you about when to hand it over."

The breath left Lilly's body and she stood frozen in the hall.

"Don't disappoint me, Ms. Burkstrom, because if you do, you won't like it."

Fear, like an evil snake, wrapped itself around her heart, squeezing it. When would this nightmare end? What was worth Peter's and now her life?

Before she could open her mouth to response, he disappeared down the hall.

"Hey, Mom, you ready to leave?"

Lilly glanced down at her daughter.

"Is something wrong?"

Hearing the fright in her daughter's voice, Lilly struggled to hide her fear.

"No. Nothing's wrong. Let's go."

TEN

Jon's heart had nearly stopped when he got the call from Lilly. He'd been talking with Dave, Marta and their pastor when his phone rang. He'd told Dave where he was going before dashing out the door of the church like a madman.

Lilly sat in her office with Penny, Pastor Kent and his wife, Rachel, and Diego and his girlfriend. When Jon appeared in the doorway, Lilly noticed him first.

She rose. "Thanks for coming. I wanted you to meet my first success, Diego Ibarra." She motioned toward the blond woman. "And this is Tina Moore. Both Diego and Tina work for the Department of Agriculture here in the state. I was telling them about our success yesterday. We're discussing how to transplant our success to other parts of the state."

Jon noticed Penny, who watched with keen interest. The plea in Lilly's eyes told him not to question her about her phone call in front of her daughter.

Jon offered his hand to Diego. "So you're the guy who inspired this ministry."

Diego smiled. "Who would've guessed a hostile, would-be gang member could've inspired this?"

"God knew," Pastor Kent offered. "God sees the entire picture. We see only the immediate. That's why we should trust Him. He will not lead us astray."

The pastor's words rang true in Jon's heart. He wished he could see more and understand what was going on. The only thing he knew was that they needed to find this guy after Lilly.

"What are you doing here?" Penny asked. "You coming to lunch with us?"

Jon knew an opening when he saw one. "I am. We had so much fun yesterday that I wanted to do it again today."

Penny glowed. "All right."

Lilly's shoulders sagged.

The group moved to a small Mexican restaurant a half a block from the church. Jon sat next to Lilly.

"Thank you," she whispered after everyone had ordered lunch.

"What happened?" Jon asked.

While everyone at the table engaged in lively conversation, Lilly explained what happened when she was on her way to the children's church service. "He wants me to give something over to him. I wanted to ask him what, but it was a one-way conversation."

Jon pulled the booking photo he'd printed earlier from the inside pocket of his sports coat. "Is this the guy, Lilly?"

She studied the photo and shook her head no. "That's not him."

Jon put the photo back into his pocket, disappointed that this wasn't their guy. "He might be after those invoices." He glanced around the table. Penny happily chatted with Diego. "The guy said he would contact you?"

She nodded.

"Okay. When he does, you ask him what he wants. Make him be as specific as you can. You want to have him name what he wants. That will help."

The waiter placed a plate of enchiladas in front of Jon. He moved on to Lilly, setting a chile relleno before her.

"When will it end?" she asked. She stared at her plate.

"Lilly, remember what your pastor just said. You see only the now. You can't see how this will work out. I never thought I'd have a life after my family died. But since that terrible time I've found myself in situations where I've been able to comfort others who'd lost loved ones. I even had the doctor who treated my daughters ask me if I would work with a family whose son had been diagnosed with the disease that killed my girls.

"I told him no, but God wouldn't let me stick my head in the sand. After reading the part in Second Corinthians where Paul told the Corinthians to comfort those with the comfort they'd received, I knew I couldn't walk away. It wasn't easy to face them, but I felt their pain. I told the father that I'd tried to drink away the pain, but it hadn't worked. God was the only source. He gives the comfort." Jon shook his head. "I always thought I was better at putting away the bad guys, but I think that dad was grateful to me for talking about the pain. When he cried, I told him it was okay."

Lilly lips trembled as she gave him a smile. "That dad was right."

Jon pulled back. "What?"

"If a strong man like you needs to lean on God, what makes the rest of us weaklings think we can do everything ourselves? You're a good example."

Lilly had touched his heart in a way no one else ever had.

"Do you think that's a good plan, Lilly?" Diego asked.

Lilly looked down the table. "What?"

"Your writing a proposal about using church land to plant gardens to help the surrounding community?" replied Diego.

"Uh, that sounds like a great idea," said Lilly.

Diego gave Pastor Kent a smile. Jon knew his and Lilly's conversation hadn't gone unnoticed. When he looked around the table, Penny grinned. He could protest about what they were thinking, but that would only exacerbate matters.

Jon's cell phone vibrated. He pulled it from his shirt pocket and looked at the number. Dave.

"Hey, partner. What can I do for you?" Jon asked.

"I got a call from one of the guys on Peter's team at the armored car business. He wants to talk to us."

"Give me the address and I'll meet you there."

Dave gave him an address in the northern part of the city.

Hanging up, Jon said, "I've got to go." He turned to

Lilly and whispered, "Check with your neighbor before you go inside your house. She'll know if anyone's stopped by."

Lilly nodded.

A thousand thoughts raced through Jon's brain as he drove to the address Dave had given him. Whoever had killed Peter Burkstrom was getting desperate. He'd gone from searching different places to letting Lilly see him to threatening her. She needed to come to the police station today and see if she could ID the man who'd threatened her.

In addition to that, tomorrow he'd call the companies whose invoices had appeared on Penny's digital picture frame. They'd be able to tell him what the materials were used for and if there was anything unusual about the invoices or changes from the original invoice.

Jon saw Dave's car and pulled up behind it. The older neighborhood housed working families. The yards were carefully tended and each house was kept in good repair. Jon walked to the front door of the house Dave had told him about and knocked on the door. Al Zeller, one of the men from Peter's armored car team, answered the door and led Jon to the living room.

"Al, why don't you tell my partner what you just told me?" Dave urged.

Al sighed. "On Friday we were finishing our run. I had just left the money in the store when I saw the guy who'd been hounding Peter at the armored car lot. He asked me if I would meet him after my shift and have a drink. He claimed he was a good friend of Pete's and needed some information. I told him that I couldn't. The next day he shows up at my daughter's soccer game. He wasn't so friendly the next day."

"What did he want?" Jon asked.

"He demanded to know if Pete had ever talked about his old job and if he'd ever mentioned something he took from that job. I told the guy that Pete had said nothing, and that if he showed up again, I was going to call the cops. The guy didn't like my reaction, but I don't want anyone messing around with my kids."

"You said this happened Friday?" Dave asked.

Al nodded. "Yeah, it did. I talked myself out of calling the cops, but then the more I thought about it, the more it bothered me. I decided to call you since I had your card."

Their suspect must be desperate. He'd broadened his circle of people he harassed. "Was there anything unusual about the man?" asked Jon.

"He had hard eyes. Must've had a bad case of acne when he was a kid, because only a mother could love that face. And he had a tattoo on his right forearm."

"What was it of?" Jon asked.

"Some sort of snake," said Al.

Jon pulled the booking photo from his pocket. "Is this the guy?"

Al shook his head. "No."

Jon leaned forward, resting his elbows on his knees. "If you see the guy anywhere, call 911. We want to get this guy."

Al nodded. "Okay."

Jon and Dave walked out to their cars.

"What happened with Lilly this morning?" Dave asked.

"Our guy ambushed her at church. He demanded that she give him what Pete took."

"The invoices?" Dave asked.

"I don't know. I'm going to find out tomorrow what those items on the invoices were for, but today I want to take Lilly down to the station and see if she can ID the guy. Could we leave Penny with you and Marta?"

Dave clapped Jon on the back. "You've just made my daughters' day. I guess we'll get another lesson in gardening. The girls are talking about putting a garden in our backyard." He shook his head. "You know what a pushover I am for the girls. I never thought I'd have a career as a farmer."

"They have your number," Jon agreed. "I'll meet you at Lilly's in about forty minutes."

"I'll call and warn the wife."

As he drove to her house, Jon called Lilly and told her what had happened with one of Peter's team members at the armored car company. "Describe to me the man who grabbed your arm in the hall at church this morning."

"Black hair, long enough to be pulled back in a ponytail. His face was pockmarked, as if he had a bad case of acne as a teen."

"What about his eyes? What color?" Jon quizzed, pressing.

"Black. And dead."

"Okay. I want you to come with me to the police station to see if we can get a name on this guy. Dave has volunteered to have Penny spend the afternoon with his girls. They're talking about putting a garden in the backyard. Penny could offer advice."

"More like direct the thing."

"I'll see you in ten."

Hanging up, he prayed, "Lord, keep Lilly and Penny safe. Give us the direction we need."

Lilly sat before the open book. The mug shots seemed to blur together. Jon worked at his desk. He glanced up.

"Did you find something?"

She let out a sign. "No."

He stood and walked over to where she sat.

"It's discouraging that this many people have police records," she said.

"Would you like for me to call the sketch artist? You can describe the man's face to her?"

She glanced at the two books of mug shots that rested on Dave's desk. He had a picture of the twins sitting beside his computer terminal. "I'll keep looking. Maybe we won't have to do that."

He went back to working on his computer. This detective, a man with a past filled with pain and tragedy, had an inner strength that amazed her.

She went back to looking for the man who'd appeared at the church this morning. An hour later, she hadn't found his mug shot.

"Let me call in our sketch artist. I want to get a picture of this guy out to the officers on patrol. I don't want him on the loose." Jon picked up the phone and made the call.

While they waited, Lilly called to check on Penny.

Marta answered the phone. "They're out in the back with Dave, deciding on the best place to put the garden."

"I'm sorry. I didn't mean to create work for you," Lilly answered.

"Are you kidding? I am so excited that the girls want to do this. They have so much energy and anything that helps drain them or keep them occupied is a blessing." She laughed. "It also gives Dave a good reason to be with the girls. We'll all benefit."

Lilly's guilt eased.

"Have you been able to identify the man?"

"No. Jon's calling in a sketch artist to help."

"Would you like to talk to Penny?" Marta asked.

"Yes."

A minute or two later Penny picked up the phone and told her mother what they were doing.

"Do you mind staying a little while longer?" Lilly asked.

"No. We're making plans. Take your time." Penny hung up.

Lilly glanced at the handset of the phone.

"What's wrong?" Jon's voice broke into her thoughts.

"My daughter just hung up on me."

"Isn't that what happens at the end of a conversation?"

Lilly felt stupid. "Yes, but—"

"But?"

"It's like she brushed me off." For some reason, Lilly felt tears threaten. "I know she didn't. It's just that my baby sounded like she didn't need me." She laughed. "Doesn't that sound stupid?"

"You're under stress, Lilly. Give yourself a break." He pulled up a chair beside hers and caught her hand. "She's a great kid. You've done a good job."

This man touched her heart in a way that made her want to confide her deepest hurts. She'd had a few good friends in her life, but, she thought, with time she and Jon could become the best of friends. "There are days when I think she runs circles around me and all I can do is ask God for wisdom."

He shook his head, a grin curving his lips. "I can believe that. Yesterday she ordered us all around with the voice of a pro."

"I'd like to say she got that from Pete, but the fact is she got it from me. I got it from my mother."

"Passing the buck?"

The door to the squad room opened and Lilly glanced over her shoulder. The woman who walked in stood only five feet high. Her long, blond hair was pulled back into a ponytail.

"Hey, Jon. You needed me?" the woman asked.

"I do, Cass. I need you to work with Ms. Burkstrom here and come up with a picture of the suspect."

Cass shook Lilly's hand and sat down. "Okay I'm going to ask you a series of questions and you'll guide me with your answers."

"Okay." said Lilly.

* * *

Jon logged into his e-mail, hoping the detective in Flagstaff had located the other man they wanted to interview. Scrolling through his e-mail, he found one from the Flagstaff PD. He opened it. The detective in Flagstaff had interviewed the other man of interest and had attached the report of the interview to the e-mail.

Jon opened the attachment. This detective's comments echoed what the detective in Cortez had said. Peter Burkstrom had treated his men right and had helped them whenever he could.

Leaning back in his chair, Jon tried to put the pieces of the puzzle together. Peter Burkstrom had run away from his responsibilities as a husband, had disappeared for a couple of years, then had reappeared, wanting to get to know his daughter.

He'd been a hard worker, working his way up the chain of command at his construction job, which meant that Adam Finley hadn't been honest with Jon. If Burkstrom had been with Painted Desert Construction long enough to work his way up to a managing position, then Finley would've had to know him.

Tomorrow he needed to go talk to Finley and get the entire story, and not the nonsense the man had spouted the other day.

"Detective, I think we're finished here," Cass called out.

Jon looked up at the sketch pad that Cass held up. The man who looked back at Jon had a hard edge. He suddenly had the feeling that this guy wasn't some gangbanger. This guy was a pro.

"That's the guy?" he asked Lilly.

Lilly nodded her head.

He could understand why this man made Lilly nervous. "Thanks, Cass."

"Sure thing." Cass ripped off the sketch and handed it to him.

Jon pulled the case file folder from under the papers on his desk and opened it. Inside was the grainy photo taken from the video tape at Peter's apartment. He compared the two. He held it up to the two women.

"Lilly, is this the same man?"

She studied the picture. "Yes."

Cass studied the photo. "There's similarity."

Jon made copies of the sketch and took them to the watch commander, explaining that if any unit spotted the man, they were to note where he was but not to apprehend him. They were also to contact Jon or his partner.

When he got back to his desk, Lilly was still sitting in Dave's chair. When she looked up and met his gaze, Jon knew then he'd fallen in love, again. And hard. It nearly knocked him off his feet.

"You ready?" he asked.

She didn't look at him. "Yes."

It seemed like the drive to Dave's house took hours. Lilly said nothing. He wanted to say…what? His feelings were out of control. He hadn't meant to fall in love. That certainly would reassure her. From what she'd told him about her ex, her experiences with love hadn't been anything to put into a romance novel.

He pulled up to Dave's house. She reached for the door handle.

"Lilly."

She turned toward him.

He wanted to apologize for his heart, but he couldn't. "I'm sorry we first doubted you when you told us about Pete and his revelation that his untimely death would be no accident. But you were the ex-wife. A lot of people have axes to grind."

Her lips curved into a smile. "It's okay. It sounded far-fetched to me, too. I felt stupid saying anything. I just repeated what he told me."

He nodded. Glancing down, he saw the copy of the sketch she'd directed. Handing it to her, he said, "Show this picture to Penny. She needs to know this is the guy we're looking for. Tell her that if he approaches her, she is to run, screaming at the top of her lungs."

"I'll do that."

They walked to the front door of the house. When they entered, Dave was standing in the foyer, talking on the phone. "We'll be there." He hung up. "That was Mrs. Zeller. Her husband went out to get a newspaper. That was close to three hours ago. He hasn't returned home. She's afraid."

Jon's gut said Mrs. Zeller had a good reason to be fearful. He glanced at Lilly. Her expression told him that she knew the missing man had something to do with her situation.

He turned to her. "I'd like for you to stay here with Marta and the girls while we go out and investigate this. Would you do that?"

Lilly swallowed.

"Penny's enjoying herself," Dave noted. "And the girls are still trying to plan a garden for our backyard. Your help is needed."

"Yes, please do help," Marta added.

Lilly looked across the living room and out into the backyard where the girls were pacing from one end to the next. "Sure. I'll lend my hand to the effort."

Relief swept through Jon. "We won't be long, and then I'll drive you and Penny home."

Marta put her arm around Lilly's shoulders. "Let's go direct our girls."

"We're taking my car," Dave said.

Jon frowned at his partner.

"From the look on your face, you won't be paying attention," Dave explained, "and I'd like to make it back to my family in one piece."

Jon wanted to argue with him, but swallowed his protest. Dave was right. He was dazed and confused. He kept tripping over his feelings. This was something he'd never experienced before. How had this happened?

ELEVEN

"Something's not right," Jon muttered as they drove to the Zellers' house.

Dave glanced at him. "It's like we're chasing our tails. And the closer we get to the heart of this matter, the more things go wrong."

Leaning against the door, Jon stared out the windshield. "That's it. We must be on the right track. We're getting blowback."

"Okay, so what's the right track? Are we're talking about things at the construction company or the armored car place?"

Jon wondered the same thing himself. "Nothing seems consistent. But we have a man searching out information that Peter had. I wish we knew who he was."

Dave turned down the last street to the Zellers' place. "You submit that booking photo to the state database and the FBI?"

"Not yet. I was waiting on our database. When we get back, I'll check and see if there've been any hits."

They pulled up to the Zellers' house and the front door opened. Mrs. Zeller hurried out to meet them.

"Is your husband still missing?" Jon asked.

"I told him not to challenge that man. He was so creepy, but Al didn't want him near our kids. Said Peter told him the guy was muscle, and not to mess with him. When I asked him about it, he just told me to call the cops if he was around the kids." She looked down at her hands. "I knew Al knew more, but—"

Jon walked her back into the house and guided her to the sofa. "Tell us what happened."

"Al was going for a newspaper. That's all. He left right after you talked to him. He has not come back. I drove down to the convenience store, but he never showed up there."

"Did he walk or take a car?" asked Jon.

She shook her head, sobs overtaking her.

Jon waited a moment. "Mrs. Zeller, whatever you can tell us, it will help."

"Dad took his car," a little boy, who was probably eight or nine, piped in because his mother couldn't stop crying.

"What does your dad's car look like?" Dave asked.

"It's black, with a green stripe on the side. It's a Honda Civic," said the boy.

Jon pulled the sketch from his pocket and showed it to Mrs. Zeller. "Is this the guy?"

She looked at the paper and nodded.

"That's him," the boy answered.

"Thanks." Dave leaned close and whispered, "I'm proud you know that information. Now, can you tell me the name of a neighbor or maybe your grandmother or grandfather so we can call them to come and help?"

"Grandma and Grandpa live in Denver. Mrs. Lee, next door, sometimes babysits us."

Dave left to ask the neighbor to stay with the family while the police looked for Mrs. Zeller's husband.

Jon called in the information on the missing man. After the neighbor came over with Dave, the detectives left and talked to the owner of the convenience store that Mrs. Zeller had mentioned. After a little questioning, the owner admitted that he'd seen Al talking to a man. They both got in Al's car and left. Jon showed him a copy of the sketch Lilly had worked on. The man IDed the guy.

Dave backed the car out of the parking place. "We've got a lot of threads, Jon, but the picture isn't coming into focus."

"What did Pete do or have that made him the target? And whatever it was, killing him didn't get the killer what he wanted. He's still after it."

"Those invoices?" Dave asked.

"Yeah, I think that's it. Let's go back to the station and look at them again."

Caren and Connie had decided what vegetables they wanted to plant in the backyard.

"Now understand, what we just harvested can't be planted until the spring," Lilly informed them.

The girls' expressions fell. "Why?"

"Fall and winter. It's going to be too cold for those

vegetables to grow, but we can make all the plans now. Then in late March and early April, you can start preparing the soil."

Caren frowned. "That's a lot of work."

Lilly hid her smile. Glancing at Marta, Lilly saw that she also fought a smile.

"I'll help," Penny offered. "It's fun."

Caren and Connie walked out the back door. Penny followed, talking about what help she could give.

"You have wonderful girls." Lilly fingered her coffee cup.

"Would you like some more coffee?" Marta asked.

"Thanks."

Marta moved to the coffeepot and brought it back to the table. She poured them both fresh cups. "You know, I never thought I'd see Jon look at a woman the way he looks at you."

Lilly's head snapped up and her cheeks flooded with color. She opened her mouth to deny those words, but the understanding in Marta's eyes invited confidences. "I guess from my expression you can tell I'm as confused about *this*—" she waved her hand "—as Jon."

Marta put a spoonful of sugar into her cup. "I can understand that. Your ex was just killed."

Lilly nodded. "Pete and I had become friends again. I grieve for him, but my heart seems to have a mind of its own. I know that sounds silly. But these feelings for Jon just blindsided me and I don't know what to do with them."

"I think Jon probably feels the same way. Give

yourself time. You might also pray about it. God brings beauty out of ashes."

Lilly stared at Marta. Was that what this was? She didn't doubt that God could bring forth something out of tragedy and sadness, but she couldn't think about the future now. All she wanted was the crazy man terrorizing their lives caught and things to return to normal.

Jon looked at the abandoned car. The police had found Al Zeller's car about a mile from the convenience store. The keys were in the ignition. The patrolman had identified the car when he discovered two youths trying to steal it.

Mrs. Zeller hadn't taken the news well.

Jon couldn't shake the feeling that things had accelerated to warp speed and something would break loose in a matter of hours. And he didn't feel right about leaving Penny and Lilly alone after they left Dave and Marta's house.

"How are you going to explain your plan to Lilly?" Dave asked once they'd hopped back into his car. "I'll go with your gut, but I don't know if she'll buy it."

Rubbing his hand over his mouth, Jon said, "I think we can sell having Penny spend the night with your girls. They've become fast friends."

"I'll buy that. What about Penny's mom? You think she'll buy that?"

Jon knew he couldn't let Lilly face this situation alone. He wouldn't sleep at all if he didn't know she was safe. "I'll convince her, no matter what it takes."

A smile curved Dave's lips.

"What?" Jon demanded.

"Nothing."

"You're lucky you stayed on the right side of the law, 'cause you can't lie worth spit."

"Sorry, buddy, but I saw you smile yesterday. Thought it would never happen again." Dave pulled the car into the driveway of his house. "You actually laughed at the way Penny bossed my girls around. Last night, when we said our prayers, Caren thanked Jesus for Uncle Jon's laughter." Dave turned off the engine and got out of the car.

If Dave had hit him with a two-by-four, Jon wouldn't have been more shocked. He realized that he'd laughed yesterday without thinking about it and with ease, enjoying Penny's performance.

Dave knocked on the passenger window. "C'mon."

Shaking off his bewilderment, Jon got out of the car. Walking into the front room, he saw Marta and Lilly standing at the kitchen table.

"Did they find the man who disappeared?" Lilly asked.

Jon entered the kitchen and explained what had happened.

Lilly fell back into a chair. The news consumed her. When she met Jon's gaze, he knew he could convince her.

"It might be a good idea if Penny spent the night here. A final sleepover before school starts. The girls mentioned some sort of sleepover yesterday after the harvesting. I think that would be an excellent idea."

Lilly's eyes narrowed. "Is there another reason why you are promoting a sleepover?"

Jon moved to the kitchen table and sat down beside her. Marta had disappeared, leaving the two of them alone. "Can you trust me, Lilly? I think it would be safer for Penny if she stayed here with Dave and Marta."

Silence ruled for a few moments; then Lilly nodded her head. "I think you're right."

Hiding his surprise, Jon continued. "I can drive you and Penny home, and then you both can get your things and spend the night here. I think Penny would probably like—"

She held up her hand. "Wait just a minute, Detective Littledeer."

He tried not to wince at her use of his last name.

Her index finger wagged back and forth. "I am not going to spend the night here. I agree Penny should. But I am not letting anyone run me out of my home."

"It's the same principle with you, Lilly. There's danger. We don't know what happened to Mr. Zeller…or your ex-husband. Someone wants something you have. He's already told you that he wants what your husband took. It's foolhardy to stay by yourself."

"What seems foolhardy to me is not to be where this guy could call me or get in contact with me." Lilly's jaw clenched and he suspected she was ready for another round of arguments. He had an aunt who, the more you warned her, the more contrary she became. His uncle had complained more than once about his wife's defiant streak.

"Okay."

Her mouth fell open.

"We'll go to your house, get Penny's things and come back here. On the way back to your house after we drop off Penny, we'll stop by my house and get my toothbrush, since I'll be spending the night at your place."

"Y-you can't," she sputtered.

"I can and I will."

"I can call Zoe. She'll stay with me."

"Fine, but I'm going to be there, too."

She opened her mouth to protest.

He rested his hand on hers. "Lilly, if anything happened to you tonight, I wouldn't be able to forgive myself. And this time I have the ability to prevent harm. You bet your life I'm going to do it." He didn't wait for Lilly's response. He called Penny inside and explained to her what she was doing tonight. Lilly called Zoe.

"Really?" Penny squealed.

The twins joined her in voicing excitement.

"Wow, Mom! How come Penny gets to spend the night?" Connie asked.

All the adults fell silent.

"Because," Marta explained, "Lilly and I talked and decided that after the wonderful job you three girls did yesterday, you deserved a treat. I'm glad you like it, and since school starts next week, this is a good time for a sleepover."

Penny caught her mother's hand. "Let's go."

* * *

Lilly kissed Penny goodbye. Her daughter hadn't hesitated for a moment as she'd walked into the twins' bedroom. She climbed in the front seat of Jon's car, awed by how quickly her daughter had taken to Caren and Connie.

"I'm kinda amazed how quickly the girls have become close," she confessed.

Fifteen minutes later Jon turned into a new town house complex just south of downtown, a series of adobe homes connected to each other. Lilly knew this complex had been built within the last year. Obviously, Jon had moved here from the home he'd shared with his family.

He pulled up to the last town house and parked. "Come inside while I get my toothbrush."

She followed him inside. The living room was neat. On the coffee table lay a large black Bible. Glancing around the room, she saw several Navajo baskets on the bookcases and on an end table. But it was the picture on the mantel that stopped her. It was a picture of his wife and daughters. Lilly slowly walked toward the fireplace. Roberta had been a beautiful woman, with long, black hair, deep brown eyes and a wonderful smile as she held her youngest. Beside her sat the other girl. She had shoulder-length hair, bangs and eyes that twinkled with mischief.

"That was taken the day before we knew about Wendy's disease," he quietly told her.

Hearing him talk about his daughters made her heart ache. She could understand how hard it had been for him. Pointing to the older girl, she said, "She was a beautiful little girl."

He picked up the picture. "She had an adventurous heart, and it got her in trouble with her mother. My little princess."

"And she made her papa proud."

He grinned. "There were a lot of times I never told Roberta what she did. Wendy could wrap me around her little finger." He set the picture down. "I can look at them now and remember the joy their lives brought to me." His gaze met hers.

Her heart wanted to give him comfort. She touched his cheek. His hand covered hers and held on.

Neither said anything for a few moments. There were no words, only recognized pain.

He caught her gaze again. "Thank you."

She knew to what he referred.

"Let's go back to your house," he said softly.

They didn't speak as they drove back to Lilly's house. Jon pulled into the driveway. As he got out of the car, he held up his hand, then crossed the street to Sandra Tillman's house.

The woman answered on the first knock. Jon talked with her for a few minutes, then rejoined Lilly.

Lilly tried not to laugh. "What did you ask her?"

"I wanted to know if anyone suspicious had been up and down this street tonight. She told me she didn't see anyone."

Lilly pulled her key out of her purse. "Did you tell her you were guarding me tonight?"

"I did. And I emphasized that it was police protection. I told her your friend would be with us. I asked her to keep an eye out for anything odd on the street."

Lilly unlocked the door. "You know you'll have an adoring fan once this is over."

He followed her into the house. He nodded as he scanned the living room. "Let me check out everything before we relax."

There would be no stopping him. She motioned him to go.

Lilly put her purse on one of the end tables. Her mind filled with images of Jonathan Littledeer, of him holding his daughter, talking with Sandra Tillman, of the look of pain in his eyes when he remembered his little girls.

He was not only handsome with his heart of gold, but he was a man who fought for justice. And he had two adamant defenders with the twins.

"It's all clear," he said, entering the living room. He looked at the couch. "I'll bunk out here."

She opened her mouth to protest, but he held up his hand. "I'm the cop. We play it my way."

She felt foolish having him guard her, but judging from his comments, he wasn't going to change his mind.

"If you want to watch TV, the remote is in the end table drawer."

"I won't need it."

"Suit yourself."

He laughed. "You've been listening to my partner's comments about me."

"About you being hardheaded?" She grinned at him. "Nope. That's from what I've seen myself."

As she walked down the hall, she heard his laugh. The deep, rich sound warmed her heart.

Twenty minutes later, Zoe arrived.

The smell of coffee drew Lilly down the hall. Jon stood in the kitchen, leaning against the counter.

"I hope you don't mind me making coffee," he said.

"Absolutely not. It's a treat to have someone else make it."

His grin woke her up more than the caffeine. "My cooking skills are limited to going to fast-food restaurants and getting a meal."

"Sounds good to me."

"Would you like to go out for breakfast?"

She shook her head. "No. I can make us a couple of eggs here. Besides, we wouldn't want to desert Zoe. If she woke up and found us missing, she'd panic and call the cops."

He shrugged. As she pulled out the frying pan, he asked, "Did you and Pete ever have any discussion about his job with the construction company or Sunbelt Securities?"

She thought about the few things that Pete had said to her. "He told me he was tired of moving from one place to another and never having a place to come home to every day. That was the reason he changed jobs."

Jon leaned back against the cabinets, his coffee in his hand as he thought. "That's understandable. Did he mention problems any other time with work at the construction firm or armored car company?"

"No."

Lilly quickly made them scrambled eggs and toast. She walked down the hall to check Zoe. She waved Lilly off, telling her she didn't do breakfast and stumbled to the shower.

"Zoe's not a morning person." The sound of the shower, punctuated her comments.

As she and Jon shared breakfast, it struck her that she hadn't had breakfast with a man since Peter left her.

"What?" Jon asked.

The man was too observant, she thought. "It's nothing."

"It might be important."

She didn't want to tell him what she'd been thinking, but he sat there waiting for an answer.

"It just dawned on me that us having breakfast is weird even if Zoe is down he hall. Pete was the last man I cooked breakfast for."

"Oh."

She stared down at her plate. How dumb, she told herself.

His cell phone rang. Jon pulled it out of his shirt pocket. After a few seconds, he said, "Where'd you find him?" He listened intently. "Okay. I'll be there ASAP." He hung up and put the cell phone on the table. "They found Al's body. He'd been shot and left in a deserted field south of town."

Pete wasn't the only person to die because of something they didn't know. "Someone is guarding their secrets fiercely," Lilly commented.

"I agree. That's the key."

TWELVE

"**M**om, I had such a neat time with Connie and Caren," Penny reassured Lilly. She yawned and rested her head against the front seat of the car.

"Did you get any sleep?"

"Yes."

Lilly threw her daughter a glance, then looked back out the front windshield.

"Okay. We talked and giggled. A lot."

"You might consider a nap in my office for a few minutes. It would help your yawning."

"I don't think so." Penny closed her eyes and her head slumped to the side.

Lilly pulled into the church parking lot, then parked in the space by the side door. Reaching over, she shook her daughter awake. "C'mon, sleepyhead. Let's go to my office."

Penny didn't offer any protest. She followed Lilly inside and climbed onto the sofa in her office and instantly fell asleep.

Lilly spent an hour going through the e-mails and

letters that people had sent about harvesting and dis-
tributing the vegetables in the garden. Every person
who'd worked last Saturday had submitted a glowing
report, and several people wanted more information on
how to start their own gardens. One wealthy parish-
ioner had suggested enlarging the garden program and
wanted to know if that was possible.

Lilly left her daughter sleeping in her office and
walked across the hall to show Pastor Kent the e-
mails. They discussed ways in which they could
involve more of the neighbors in the garden, helping
to prepare the ground, sow the seeds and care for the
plants. Also, they discussed if they should use more
church land to enlarge the garden or if they should
lease a remote site.

With her head filled with hope and ideas, Lilly
walked back into her office. She noticed that Penny
was no longer asleep on the sofa.

"Penny," she called out. There was no answer. Maybe her daughter had gone to the bathroom. She walked
to the ladies' restroom and checked there. It was empty.
Lilly next tried the kitchen. Sometimes her daughter
helped herself to one of the soft drinks they kept in the
fridge.

"Penny?"

There was no answer.

Lilly walked the entire length of the first floor, calling out her daughter's name. By the time she reached
the stairs leading to the second floor, panic clutched
her heart. She raced upstairs.

"Penny, where are you? C'mon, sweetheart! Now is not the time to play hide-and-seek."

No one answered her. She stepped to the window on the second-floor landing and peered out, scanning the surrounding area. She saw a car turn down a side street. From its direction, she thought it might've come from the church parking lot.

She shot down the stairs. "Pastor Kent! Pastor Kent!" she screamed.

Pastor Kent and his secretary, Joy, raced into the hall.

"Lilly, what's wrong?" said the pastor.

"Penny's missing!" Lilly gasped between breaths.

"Wasn't she in your office?" Joy asked.

"I left her in the office while we talked about expanding the garden. Penny wouldn't have wandered off," Lilly replied.

Lilly raced into the secretary's office and grabbed the phone. She knew Jon's cell phone number by heart now. He picked up on the first ring.

"Jon!" Lilly gasped. "Penny is missing from the church!"

"I'm coming, Lilly! You sit tight," he told her.

She hung up the phone. She turned to look at Pastor Kent, then bent over and let loose with a scream.

That killer had her baby.

Why?

Why?

"What happened?" Dave asked Jon.

"Penny's missing."

Both men moved into action. Jon pulled out his weapon, checking to make sure it was loaded. He and Dave raced out of the building to their police-issue sedan.

"Let me drive," Dave commanded. "You can make calls while I drive."

Jon nodded, sliding into the passenger seat. The ride to the church was the longest one of Jon's life. His mind went into overdrive. They would have the patrol cops canvass the area around the church to see if anyone had witnessed a child in distress or any suspicious activity. Maybe they could find clues in the parking lot.

When Dave pulled up to the side door at the church, Jon threw open the car door, jumped out of the car and sprinted inside. He found Lilly in the pastor's office. When she spotted him, she came to her feet and threw herself into his arms. He hugged her and his eyes drifted closed.

"Someone's taken her, Jon." Lilly spoke into his ear. "Someone has my baby."

Jon's heart felt as if it were torn and bleeding. "I'll do my best, Lilly." He pulled back and cupped her face. "We'll use every means at our disposal to try to find her."

She nodded.

He brushed his lips over hers.

The front doors to the church opened and voices filled the foyer.

Pulling back, Jon whispered, "Pray, because we need His guidance."

* * *

The church came alive with people. Uniformed officers were searching the grounds. So far they'd found no clues. Pastor Kent brought Lilly a sandwich his wife had sent. Lilly smiled weakly and took the bag. Walking back in her office, she set the bag on her desk.

She sat at her desk and prayed. "Lord, keep my baby safe. Please."

She heard a cell phone ring. It wasn't her cell phone. When it rang again, she looked around her desk. The muted sound made her think it was inside something.

She yanked out the middle drawer of her desk. It wasn't in there.

The phone continued to ring.

She tried the next drawer.

Nothing.

She tried the bottom drawer. She saw nothing but her purse. The cell phone rang again. The ring came from her purse. She unzipped the main compartment and looked inside. There beside her cell phone was another phone.

It rang again.

With trembling fingers she picked up the phone and pushed the talk button.

"Hello." Her voice shook.

"I warned you that I want what your ex-husband took. I'll trade you. The evidence for your daughter."

Fear clutched her throat.

"I don't—"

"Lady, I've got your daughter. She will die if I don't get that evidence. Keep this phone with you. I'll contact you later with instructions. Your daughter's safety depends on you."

The line went dead.

She stared down at the phone, overwhelmed.

Jon walked in the room. "Lilly?"

Lifting her head, she whispered, "He's kidnapped her."

Jon's heart jerked at the words. He squatted before her. "What did he say?"

"He said he wants what Peter took. I guess he means the information on the flash drive." Staring down at the phone she clutched in her hand, she said, "He's got my baby."

Jon placed his hand over hers. "Lilly, we are going to do everything in our power to get her back."

The wounded look in her eyes cut across his heart.

"You can't guarantee that, can you?"

"No."

She wrapped her arms around his neck and shook with her tears.

In the doorway, Jon saw Dave. He'd heard the exchange. He nodded and disappeared down the hall.

Pastor Kent moved toward them. He rested his hand on Lilly's shoulder and began to pray out loud. "Lord, keep Penny safe…"

Jon didn't hear the rest of the prayer. Instead he prayed that God would give him the wisdom to rescue

Penny and catch her kidnapper. It might be the killer himself or someone who'd been hired to recover the evidence. It didn't matter. He wanted this guy.

When the pastor finished the prayer, Jon pulled away from Lilly. "Let me have the phone for a moment to look at it."

She hesitated.

"I won't take it far. I want to see if I recognize the phone. Maybe I can ID where the phone was purchased." When she didn't move, he added, "I won't leave this room."

She handed him the phone. Studying the model, he recognized it as one available in most convenience stores in Albuquerque. He took down the serial number and gave the phone back to her.

Then he met Dave in the hall.

"Did the evidence team find anything that will tell us who this guy is? Anyone see anything?"

Dave sighed. "Nothing so far. If this guy is a pro, we're not going to find anything."

"You contacted the FBI?"

"I've notified Scott. He's coming."

Penny wasn't only missing, but she was a kidnap victim, and although she probably hadn't been taken out of the jurisdiction, it was smart to inform the Feds. Jon didn't think the kidnapper would take the child to another state. He needed her to exchange for the flash drive. With cases like these, the Albuquerque PD normally kept Scott apprised of developments.

Jon wanted to punch something to vent his frustration. "No one's perfect. The guy had to leave behind something besides the phone."

Jon walked up and down the hallway. When he reached the end of the hallway the third time, he looked up and saw a small camera pointed at the pastor's office. "We might have caught a break," he told Dave as he walked back into Lilly's office. "Where's the video feed for the camera aimed at the pastor's office?"

Pastor Kent, Lilly and Joy looked at him.

"It's in my office," Pastor Kent replied. He led everyone into his office. He logged onto the computer and brought up the security camera for the front hall.

They watched the pastor's door and saw Lilly cross into the pastor's office. About a minute later, a shadow appeared in the hall and then vanished. Less than a minute later the shadow reappeared. This time the camera caught one side of a man's face. They also saw Penny's legs hanging over his arm.

"Stop it," Jon commanded. "Let's make a copy of that and give it to our evidence team. We have at least a side shot of the man."

"What good is that?" Lilly asked, the kidnapper's prepaid cell phone still clutched in her hand.

"It gives us the height, weight, race of the man," Dave explained.

Lilly collapsed onto a chair in front of the pastor's desk.

Someone from the evidence team took the disk.

Jon talked with the team at the scene. They were

finished here. After consulting with Dave, Jon decided to go home with Lilly. Dave drove back to headquarters.

Lilly was still sitting in the chair in the pastor's office when Jon drew Lilly to her feet. "Let me take you home. We'll wait for the kidnapper's call."

She nodded and walked toward her office. Jon followed. Lilly got her purse from the desk drawer. She looked at the sofa in her office where Penny had slept. Her eyes caught sight of something on it. She walked over and moved aside one of the decorative pillows. Underneath was a ribbon. A blue hair ribbon.

"She had that in her hair when she came in this morning." Wrapping her hand around the ribbon, Lilly took a deep breath. "Maybe you should be the person who drives."

He nodded and held out his hand for her keys. Her hand shook as she surrendered the key ring, thankful Jon was here to help her.

On the way to Lilly's house, Jon stopped by the police station, hoping that one of the companies he'd contacted about the invoices on Penny's photo frame had returned his call. He left Lilly with a cup of coffee in the break room, where she was talking with one of the female officers.

He checked his voice mail; both companies had contacted him. He quickly dialed the iron company. The vice president told him that the invoice for rebar was related to an overpass constructed on State Highway 53 near the Zuni Reservation that Painted Desert

Construction bought. The company had bid on the contract two years ago. The vice president gave him the state number of the contract and filled him in on the particulars.

Jon called the other company. A concrete company. Their answers were a little less forthcoming. When Jon continued asking questions, the supervisor told him that he didn't have all the paperwork.

"Then get it," Jon replied.

"You misunderstood me, detective. There's nothing else in this file on the project."

"Let me talk to someone who can answer my questions."

"Detective, I'm telling you the paperwork for that project is not in the folder. Maybe it was misplaced or misfiled, but it isn't where it should be," the supervisor asserted.

"Who oversaw the project?"

"I don't know. It's not here in the file, where it should be."

"Why don't you let me talk to someone who can answer my questions?"

"Just a minute," snapped the supervisor.

Jon's neck itched. That meant something wasn't right.

"Detective, this is Boyd Masters. I am the head of contracts for our firm. What seems to be wrong?"

"I need information, Mr. Masters. I need the name of the person who was in charge of delivering concrete ordered by Painted Desert Construction Associates to the construction company's bridge work site off Highway

53, just south of Grants. Your assistant couldn't tell me anything. I just need to check the paperwork on the concrete you delivered to that job site."

"Why do you need this?"

"It is part of a murder investigation."

Masters became silent.

"I can get a court order to see the contract, sir," Jon barked.

"I'll have to speak with our lawyers. I'll get back to you." He hung up.

Dave walked into the squad room. "What are you doing here?"

Jon told him what he'd just discovered.

"So maybe those copies of the invoices might be proof of what?"

"I don't know, but when I take Lilly home, I'll call the state highway department and see what those invoices mean to them. Why don't you see about getting warrants to look at those invoices?"

Dave nodded. "Sounds like a plan. Scott showed up at the church. He is coming by and hopes to talk to Lilly."

"He wants to talk to her here?"

"That's the plan."

Jon went to the break room to tell Lilly. "The FBI is coming by to talk with you."

"What are they going to do?"

"In kidnap situations we let the FBI know. They don't get involved unless the victim is taken across state lines."

Her face lost all color.

"Don't lose hope, Lilly. Our guy wants what you have, and he isn't going to gamble that by not having Penny close by. Calling Scott in is a good resource for us. He's dealt with more kidnappers than I have."

She nodded. Jon guided her to his desk in the squad room and pointed to his chair. She sat in the chair, her eyes dark with worry. Keep a professional distance, his cop brain told him, but his newly reawakened heart didn't listen. He pulled up a chair and grasped her hand.

About fifteen minutes later, Scott Landers walked in the room. A little over six feet tall, he was a well-built man with massive shoulders and clear green eyes that could pierce like a laser. His brown hair was cut in a military fashion. Jon knew Scott had been in Army Intelligence before he joined the FBI.

Scott introduced himself to Lilly and listened to her story.

"So the kidnapper hasn't called you back again?" Scott asked when she finished.

"No," she replied.

He turned to Jon. "Do we know where the cell phone was purchased?"

"We're checking with the manufacturer. They've not gotten back to us."

Scott nodded. "Let me put some pressure on them and see if we can get that information ASAP." He turned to Lilly. "At this point, I just want to familiarize myself with the case. We don't get involved until we know the victim has been taken across state lines. I'll help these detectives."

She nodded.

"I'll check with my sources in the highway department and compare notes with them," Jon told Scott and Dave.

After Dave and Scott divided up the other areas to check, Jon looked at Lilly. She had that same clouded look that Roberta had had after they'd buried Rose.

He knew he needed to get Lilly home.

"Let's go, Lilly." Jon gently pulled her from the chair. He slid his arm around her waist.

"When I come up with something, I'll give your cell a call," Scott told him.

Jon nodded and guided Lilly to her car. As he drove to her house, he prayed. *Lord, touch her heart. Don't let her give up. You can heal her broken heart. Sustain her.*

And give me the wisdom to stop this evil.

His mind ran over all the information he knew, trying to come up with the key.

He knew that without his action, that little girl didn't stand a chance of surviving.

And this was an enemy he could fight, whereas the disease that killed his daughters he could do nothing to stop.

When they arrived at Lilly's house, Zoe was waiting for them. She took Lilly in her arms and walked her back to the master bedroom.

Jon hit the off button on his cell phone. He'd just finished comparing the specs of the Highway 53 bridge contract between the state and the construction company and the actual materials listed on the concrete company's invoice. They were not the same. There was also an invoice in the state's files that did not resemble the one Peter Burkstrom had a copy of. Jon had e-mailed his source copies of the invoice.

What he'd just figured out was explosive. He dialed a friend in the fraud unit of the police department. Jon explained to him what he'd uncovered.

"What it sounds like is that Painted Desert Construction shorted the state on the materials for that bridge," said his friend.

Jon's mind raced at the implications. "Which means the bridge may not be up to code."

"You got it. And it appears that the concrete wasn't up to the specifications the state wanted. In other words, the state paid for X and got Y. And depending on the conditions the bridge is exposed to, it could tumble down. If one massive freeze or flooding occurs in that area, you're minus one bridge."

It would be enough to kill for, Jon thought. "Thanks," he said, hanging up.

Excitement raced through him. He knew the key. Now who was in on the wrongdoing remained an unanswered question.

"Lilly," he called.

He walked down the hall to her bedroom. She'd disappeared down the hall a while back. The room was dark and he could see from the light in the hallway that Lilly was lying on the bed, curled around the doll that was Penny's favorite. She'd fallen asleep.

"Thank you," he whispered to Zoe. He also sent a thank-you to heaven.

He walked back into the living room.

Pulling out his cell phone, he dialed his partner. Dave needed to know what he'd discovered.

Dave answered on the first ring.

"I think I know what our killer is after."

THIRTEEN

The next morning, Jon told Lilly about the information he'd uncovered.

"The construction company your ex-husband worked for did some funny business in its dealings with the state highway department. They cheated the state by building a bridge but with substandard materials. With the concrete used, the bridge will not stand up to the weather and is in danger of collapsing with a bad snowstorm or flood."

Lilly suddenly recalled something Peter had told her while he worked at his old job, before he'd gone back to church. "I remember one weekend when Pete came for Penny. When I answered the door, he was on the phone with someone. He told the man it wouldn't last. The person on the other end said something. Pete told him it was his responsibility. When I asked him if everything was okay, he ignored the question and smiled at Penny, asking her if she was ready to go tubing."

"Do you have any idea who he was talking to?" Jon asked, pressing.

"No. He never said anything more, but sometimes in an unguarded moment, I saw something in his eyes. Regret. Worry, I don't know."

Jon looked down at his coffee. "I think you're right that something was bothering him. He kept the proof of what materials were really used in the building of the bridges, because the invoice the state highway department has is different from the one Peter put on the flash drive."

"I wonder what happened to the original invoice?" Lilly asked.

"What I want to see is the delivery order for the concrete. It will tell me who accepted the inferior materials."

Lilly stared into her coffee. Her fear for Penny's safety seemed like a bulldozer running over her. Her hands shook as she tried to take a sip of her coffee. Jon put his coffee down and took the cup from her hands, setting it by his. Standing, he wrapped his arms around her waist and pulled her close.

"I'm so afraid," she whispered into his chest.

He rested his chin on her head. "I know. When the doctors first told us about Wendy's condition, I thought we could fight our way through. Those were two of the most terrible years of my life. If I'd known the Lord then, I could've let Him comfort me. And I could've comforted Roberta. I did it alone. I tried to drown those bad memories in liquor."

She looked up at him and saw the torture in his eyes.

He glanced down at her. A poignant smile curved

his lips. "It took a little warrior named Caren to set me straight. God has taken what I lived through and allowed me to help other families in that situation. You have His hope in you now, Lilly. Rely on it." He leaned down and brushed his lips across hers.

She rested her head on his chest. Thinking about what he went through—the pain and sorrow—she realized his words about trusting God came from experience.

Suddenly the prepaid cell phone from the kidnapper rang. Zoe appeared in the hallway.

Lilly's gaze flew to Jon's. He nodded for her to pick it up.

Her fingers shook as she grabbed the phone and pressed the talk button.

"You have what I want?" said a male voice.

Her gaze locked with Jon's. "All I have is a flash drive with some invoices on it," she said softly.

"Good. I want you to go to the new city mall. You are to arrive at eleven forty-five. Go to the food court. There's a table just inside the food court that is across the bridge and in front of Mama's Tamales. Sit there and wait."

"But—" The line went dead.

"What did he say?" Jon asked.

She repeated the kidnapper's instructions.

Zoe rushed to her side.

Instantly, Jon called Dave. "We've had contact. Notify hostage rescue. I'll call Scott." He hung up, then dialed another number.

Lilly walked to the kitchen sink and emptied out her

mug. She put her coffee in the sink. "Oh, Lord," she choked out. "Give my baby strength and keep her safe."

She felt Jon's hand on her back. Turning into his embrace, she wrapped her arms around his waist. "Amen," he whispered. "Give her mother strength, too."

"Thank you," she said.

His forefinger raised her chin. "For what?"

"For being here. For praying. For being a cop who's going to help find my Penny."

He wiped away the moisture from her cheeks. "I wish there was more I could do."

"I know." Over his shoulder, Lilly saw Zoe watching them.

"But what I know is that you need to eat. Do it for Penny. You need to be able to think and have your body operate in the right way." He stepped away and opened her cabinets. "How about I make us some scrambled eggs and you toast the English muffins?" He didn't wait for a response but handed her the English muffins and went to work on making the eggs.

He was right. She'd eat. For Penny.

As he broke the eggs in to the pan, she glanced at his tall, imposing form. As he took a sip of his coffee, the morning sun outlined his stark features. He'd been a rock during this nightmare. What would she have done without him? His manner with Penny had won her heart. Was she falling in love? The thought only added to her confusion.

Zoe sat beside her, grabbed her hand and smiled.

* * *

Jon wasn't happy with the plan. He wanted to be on hand in the food court when Lilly went in, but they couldn't afford to deviate from the established plan. Zoe wasn't happy, either, and wanted to accompany Lilly. That idea was nixed. He would use the surveillance cameras that the mall already had in place to monitor the situation. Several officers would be stationed around the food court.

Jon sat before the bank of monitors in the mall's control room.

Dave entered the room. "We got a hit in AFIS."

"The FBI identified the prints?"

"Our kidnapper is George Pardue, aka Snake. He's out of Houston. He's a known hit man and enforcer." Dave held up a picture of Snake.

Jon looked at the man. Their guy had the dead eyes of a soulless man. Seeing their suspect, Jon didn't want Lilly anywhere near him. What worried him was what the suspect had done with Penny.

"Keep your eyes peeled," Jon whispered into his chin mic.

The officers stationed around the food court each checked in.

Dave sat down beside Jon. "Pardue did a stretch in the Texas prison system. He was a teen when he killed his first man. He was released when he turned eighteen. He disappeared from sight, and when he resurfaced, he was closely tied to some of the Colombian dealers. He's been around the world. Russia, Poland, Afghanistan."

"So what you're telling me is that the guy who hired Pardue has shelled out big money to cover up this bridge deal?"

Dave sighed. "This could be the tip of an iceberg."

Jon didn't like the numbers of people filing into the food court. "Where's the guy?" He glanced down at his watch.

"He's late. And there are a lot of teens wanting to eat lunch," replied Dave.

"He's watching." Jon hit his fist on the console. "But where?"

A group of about twenty elderly people walked into the food court, blocking his view of Lilly. Jon didn't wait, but dashed out of the control room.

Something was going down.

Lilly looked around at the people filing into the food court. Her stomach knotted. Looking down at her watch, she noted that the man was late. He'd said 11:45 a.m. It was 12:10 p.m.

"Mary, I can't decide what I want," an elderly woman told her friend.

"I've always loved the gyros," her friend answered.

A man appeared beside Lilly.

"Let's go," he growled.

Lilly glanced up at him. It was the guy who had accosted her at the church.

"Where's my daughter?"

"I'll take you to her. You have what I want?"

She nodded.

"Let me see."

"No. I want assurances that my daughter is okay."

He shrugged and turned to go.

Jumping to her feet, she grabbed his arm. "I want my daughter. I have what you want." She reached into her jeans pocket and drew out the flash drive.

He didn't try to take it, but nodded, grabbed her arm and led her to the back of the food court.

Panic raced through her. He was taking her out a back way. Fighting back her fear, she followed. She wouldn't be any help to her daughter if she fell apart and started sobbing. She had to keep her wits about her. As they exited the delivery doors, she prayed that Jon would see what was happening.

By the time Jon arrived at the food court, Lilly was nowhere to be seen. Turning in a circle, he scanned the area. He didn't see her anywhere.

Dave came to a stop beside Jon, along with two of the officers stationed around the food court.

"Where is she?" Dave asked.

"She was gone when I got here. Let's fan out and see if we can locate the two of them." Jon looked at his people. They all knew Lilly wasn't alone. "If you see our suspect, radio it in."

They scattered.

Jon hadn't known such fear since the doctors first told them him about his daughter's illness. Shoving it aside, he started scanning the food court again. When he spotted a table of older ladies who were chatting about the food, he asked if they had seen a woman who fit Lilly's description.

"Yes, she was at that table," one of the women answered.

"Did you see where she went?" Jon quizzed.

"A man came up and said something to her. She didn't like what he said. When he started to leave, she chased after him," said the woman.

"Which direction did they go in?"

The woman pointed to the hallway leading to the back of the food court.

He thanked the woman and sprinted down the hallway.

Lilly felt like a rag doll as the man pulled her down the back stairs and out the food-service delivery entrance. The sunlight momentarily blinded her. She stumbled. Her captor jerked her upright. He didn't say anything but continued walking.

They threaded their way around several commercial trucks. Signs on the sides of the trucks let her know that they belonged to the biggest vegetable distributor in the tristate area.

Rushing behind the tall man, Lilly dropped several of her church business cards. She wanted to leave a trail behind her so Jon would know in which direction she'd gone. She prayed the man wouldn't turn around. She felt around in her purse, found her cell phone and slipped it into the front pocket of her jeans.

They arrived at a van. Painted on the side of the van was a carpet company logo.

He jerked open the sliding door of the van and pushed her inside. She landed on her left shoulder, jamming it against the floor. The pain took her breath away.

Her captor ran around the front of the van, jumped into the driver's seat and revved the engine. In less than two seconds, he backed out of the slot, put the van in Drive and sped off. The momentum sent Lilly rolling back into a piece of equipment. Whatever it was, it forced the air from her lungs. Black spots danced before her eyes.

She struggled to maintain her grip on the here and now. After several bracing breaths, she focused on the dirty floor of the van.

Jon needed to know where she was. Reaching into her jeans pocket, she took out her cell phone and turned it on. She dialed 911. She put the phone to her thigh to muffle the sound. When she was sure the 911 operator had answered, she set the phone on the van floor, behind a bucket.

"Where are you taking me?" she asked her captor.

He didn't answer.

"You are taking me to see my daughter, aren't you? I know Penny will be frightened and I want to comfort her."

The driver stopped at a light. He turned and gave her a death stare. "Lady, shut your trap."

She opened her mouth, but his glare effectively silenced her.

No sound came from the cell phone, but Lilly

prayed that the 911 operator had caught on to what was happening and relayed the information to the proper authorities.

Lord, all things are in Your hands. Please let Jon know where I am.

Jon scanned the parking lot. The hall pointed out to him by the ladies had led to the elevator and stairs to the ground floor. He knew the guy had escaped to his car. He walked up and down the rows of cars, looking for some clue. He noticed a business card for Lilly's church lying on the ground. Picking it up, he realized immediately that Lilly had thrown in on the ground so he would know she'd been there.

He ran his hands through his hair. His walkie-talkie squawked. "Jon, come on up to the mall control room. We've got a shot of Lilly as she was dragged from the mall," said Dave.

At a run, he headed back inside to the control room. He shoved open the door to the room. "What have you got?"

Dave motioned him to the bank of monitors. On one of the cameras overlooking the parking lot Lilly appeared, being dragged by Snake. They watched as he shoved her into a van and the van pulled out of the lot.

"Can you make out the plate on the van?" asked Jon.

"No. It's too grainy."

Jon immediately radioed dispatch and ordered an ID on the van. He also radioed his team the make and model of the van and a description. "He dragged her out the food-service entrance," he noted. "How did he get through our team?"

"The place is crowded, Jon," Dave answered. "He was determined."

Jon knew his partner was right. And his gut told him why Lilly hadn't created a scene but had gone with the man. She wanted her daughter back. He turned around and listened as the other cops in the mall checked in.

He reviewed the plan in his mind. What had gone wrong? How could he have stopped what had happened?

"Yeah, I'll tell him." Dave closed his phone. "That was the captain. Apparently, Lilly dialed 911 on her cell phone so the operator could listen in, and she has kept the phone on. The cell company is trying to triangulate on the signal."

Hope sprang to life in Jon's heart. "That's the way to go, Lilly," he whispered. "Let's go and follow her cell phone signal."

Lilly's heart raced and she fought the fear trying to crush her. The van pulled off the paved road and onto a bumpy road. There were no shocks in this van and a roll of carpet shook loose, falling on her leg.

She swallowed her cry of pain. With her free foot, she tried to push the carpet off her leg and onto the van floor. It took four tries before she got the crushing weight off her leg. She rested her head back on a pile of drop cloths.

The van screeched to a stop. Her captor climbed out

and slammed the driver's door shut. Lilly wedged her cell phone behind the roll of carpet just before the side door opened.

"C'mon, lady." He didn't point a gun at her, but Lilly didn't doubt that he had one under the shirt he wore, which was untucked from his pants.

She gathered her purse and scooted toward the door. When she was close enough, he grabbed her elbow, pulling her from the van.

Glancing around, she saw that the place was some sort of road construction project. On the side of the partially built bridge sat a plain white trailer.

He steered her to the trailer door and unlocked it. "Get in," her captor instructed.

Lilly looked inside and saw Penny. She lay on a couch, not moving. Lilly raced to Penny's side. The little girl didn't move. Lilly's gaze drilled into their captor. "Did you ki—"

"Lady, she's fine. I gave her something that would knock her out for a few hours."

Lilly glared at him. "She's a little girl."

He shrugged. "I could've tied her to the chair, if you prefer that."

Looking down, Lilly saw the gentle rise and fall of her daughter's chest. Lilly brushed a few strands of hair from Penny's cheek. The relief flooding her nearly knocked her off her feet.

Their captor sat down in the chair opposite her. Holding out his hand, he said, "Now, let's see your evidence."

Lilly pulled the flash drive from her front jeans pocket and handed it to him.

Holding up the flash drive, he asked, "This is what your ex-husband had? No hidden papers or diary?"

"That's it. Pete never said anything about his work. We were divorced. And it wasn't a pleasant divorce." She didn't add that that was years ago and they'd change the tone of the relationship. "I never would have found that if my daughter…I hadn't looked at a bunch of pictures on this digital frame and seen the papers. I think what you want is there."

Pulling out his cell phone, he dialed a number. "I've got what you want." The man looked at her. "Okay." He hung up the phone. "Let me see your purse," he commanded.

Lilly didn't like it, but she handed over her purse. He searched the purse, then handed it back to her. "Stand up."

"Why?"

"I'm going to pat you down, in case you're wired."

She slowly came to her feet. He quickly ran his hands over her. Satisfied she wasn't wired, he said, "Make yourself comfortable."

"Are you going to let us go?" she asked.

He didn't bother answering.

Lilly knew that she wasn't going to sit by and let this man kill her and her daughter. She would fight. She didn't know how, but she vowed she would.

Jon sat in their police-issue car, waiting for the phone company to call back with the location of the cell phone broadcast. Dave sat beside him. They didn't say anything, but both knew that Lilly and Penny were more than just victims in this case. Lilly and Penny had slipped under Jon's guard, touching his heart, which hadn't felt anything since he'd buried his wife and daughters.

Dave didn't press him with any questions. Questions Jon couldn't have answered.

The radio sprang to life. "Jon, we've got a hit. The phone company triangulated on the signal and determined its location. On the interstate, just north of the city."

"You got a street address?" asked Jon.

"No. It's coming from an undeveloped area. Around fifteen miles north of the city. Looks like maybe on State Highway 44."

"Got it. Have units from the highway patrol meet us at the turnoff of I-25 and State Highway 44."

Jon hung up and started the car. Dave put the flashing light on the dash. They were going to make it through the city in record time.

As Jon drove, Dave picked up the radio and coordinated with the other units.

"Read me the rap sheet on our kidnapper," Jon asked when Dave finished with the arrangements.

"Let's see. Pardue killed his first man when he was fourteen, his stepfather. Apparently the guy beat Pardue senseless. The kid killed him when he was drunk." Dave reread the part about the man's association with different crime syndicates and families throughout the world. "So what's a guy of this caliber doing messing around with Pete Burkstrom?"

"That's the question burning in all our guts."

The knock on the door of the trailer made Lilly jump. Snake, her captor, opened the door. A well-dressed man walked into the trailer. He didn't look at her. "Where is it?"

Snake pulled the flash drive from his shirt pocket. The other man nodded and disappeared outside.

Lord, don't let him find that phone, Lilly prayed silently.

She ran her fingers through Penny's hair, grateful her daughter was okay. Suddenly Penny's eyes fluttered open. It took a moment, but her daughter smiled.

"You're here!"

"Of course I'm here." Lilly fought to keep the fear out of her voice. Penny needed to stay calm. "Did you think I wouldn't come?"

"I was so scared. I kept praying that Jesus would send Jon to come and rescue me. Is he coming?"

Lilly put a finger to her lips. "Shhh." She nodded yes. Penny's fear subsided.

"Now, I don't know what is going to happen or when Jon will get here, but if I tell you to do something, you do it. Don't question me. Understand?"

Penny nodded. "I prayed for that man, too."

"What man?"

"The man who grabbed me. I told him he needed Jesus."

Lilly blinked several times. "What did he say?"

"He didn't say anything. Just got this weird look on his face. He was nicer after that. He gave me a soft drink and a candy bar. I got sleepy after that."

Lilly pulled her daughter close, amazed at her actions. Out of the mouths of babes came such truth.

Finley pulled his laptop from the backseat of his car, put it on top of the trunk, turned it on and inserted the flash drive. Twenty thumbnails came up. He clicked on one picture. It was of a little girl at a water park. "What's this?"

"Try another one." Snake pointed to another thumbnail. "The ex said it was mixed in with pictures of her daughter."

Finley clicked on another thumbnail. It was a copy of the invoice for the concrete really used in the bridge project Burkstrom had supervised. Too bad Burkstrom got religious and wanted things set right.

Finley cursed. He clicked on another thumbnail. Another invoice. "What he copied could put me out of business. Why he suddenly became such a choir boy, I don't know."

"Maybe he wanted some insurance to protect himself."

Finley glared at the man. "I don't need your opinion."

"You got what you want?" Snake asked.

"I'll destroy this." Finley pulled out the flash drive, dropped it on the ground, and stepped on it, crushing it in the dust with the heel of his boot. He put his laptop back in the car. "You'll have your final payment when you dispose of the witnesses inside the trailer."

"I'll need my final payment before I finish," Snake calmly replied.

Finley frowned. "I won't cheat you."

"This is business, Finley. I'm paid, and then I'll finish the job."

The other man threw out his chest. "How do I know you won't let those people go?"

"You don't. I can walk away now and let the chips fall where they may."

Finley glared at him.

Snake said nothing.

"I'll go by the office and make the money transfer. I'll give you a call in a few minutes, when it is done." Finley got into his car and sped out of the construction site.

Snake turned around and headed for the trailer. Finley might not like his methods, but he'd been shorted only on one job. And that individual had got what he deserved.

Jon pushed the cruiser to its limits. The radio came on. "I got a white sedan speeding away from a construction site. He's headed south on State Highway 44, just below Santo Domingo Pueblo. He's flooring it."

Jon didn't know who was in the car, but he intended to stop it. As he turned onto State Highway 44, he asked, "You with me, Dave, if I stop whoever this is?"

"What do you have in mind?"

"Putting on the light and siren and chasing this car down."

Dave picked up the handset and radioed what they were about to do.

"See if we can get the tribal police to join in," Jon instructed.

As Dave radioed the request, their suspect flew over a hill, heading for I-25. Jon turned the cruiser around, his siren blaring. The person in the white car sped up. As he approached the merging lane to I-25, he swerved to take an unpaved side road.

He didn't make the turn. The white sedan skidded, hit a large boulder and flipped twice in the air. It came to rest on its wheels. Smoke poured out of the open hood.

The cruiser skidded to a stop. Both Jon and Dave jumped out. Jon went to the driver's side of the white sedan, opened the door, hit the release on the seat belt and pulled the man from the vehicle.

Three seconds later the engine exploded, sending the sedan several feet off the ground. Jon covered his head, but felt a piece of burning metal knock him in the back. Dave ran over and patted Jon's back, putting out the sparks on his shirt.

"You okay?" Dave asked.

Jon didn't feel anything besides an urgency to find Lilly and Penny. "I'm fine."

They looked down at the man. Adam Finley. The man had a gash on his head, and was bleeding and unconscious.

"I'll stay here," Dave said. "You go get Lilly and Penny."

"I'll call for help," Jon yelled as he raced back to their cruiser. *Lord, let me get there before anything goes wrong.*

Snake walked back into the trailer. Lilly could read nothing on his face. He sat down in the chair opposite her.

He said nothing.

"Are you going to let us go?" Lilly asked. "That flash drive was what that man wanted, wasn't it?"

Snake leaned back. "I'm waiting for him to call back."

That didn't sound good. "I promise you that Penny and I have no idea what is going on. Let us go."

"I'm waiting."

Lilly's eyes scanned the trailer for some sort of weapon she could use to hit her captor with.

Suddenly the sound of cars speeding up and stopping outside the trailer filled the air. The sound of a helicopter's blades joined the noise.

Snake looked out the window of the trailer.

"This is the Albuquerque police, the New Mexico state police and the Santo Domingo Pueblo tribal police. The trailer is surrounded. Send out the woman and child. Then come out with your hands up." The command came through a bullhorn.

Snake turned back to Lilly and Penny.

"You're in trouble," Penny said.

Lilly's eyes widened in horror.

Snake opened the trailer door and yelled, "I'll send out the little girl, but the woman comes with me. I want a private plane. I'll release the woman when I board the plane."

"No deal," shouted the officer on the bullhorn.

"Make up your mind. I can hold both females hostage."

"We caught the guy who hired you. He's on his way to the hospital now," yelled the officer.

Lilly raced to the trailer door. "Jon, I'll go with him if he'll let Penny go," she shouted.

Snake pushed her aside. "I'll give you three minutes to decide what to do." He slammed the door shut.

Ben Narvaiz of the state police and Cruz Romero, an Inter-tribal Indian officer, approached Jon.

"One of my men," Cruz said, "is nestled in those hills beyond the road. He's got a perfect shot. He can take the man out."

Jon didn't want to risk it, but Lilly's chances of survival would go down if she left here with Snake.

"If we play along with the kidnapper, we can get the little girl out. Then we can take out the kidnapper," Ben Narvaiz added.

Jon thought about it for a moment. "How good is your sharpshooter?"

Cruz met Jon's eyes. "He's the best I've ever seen. Before he joined our force, he was a sniper with the U.S. Army."

That was all Jon needed to know. He had worked with snipers when he was in the army and didn't doubt this man could get the job done. "Okay. Let's go with your plan."

Cruz radioed his sharpshooter. When things were ready, he nodded.

"Snake. You've got a deal," yelled the officer on the bullhorn.

There was no immediate response. Just when Jon thought things were going south, the trailer door opened and Penny walked out. She glanced over her shoulder. Lilly appeared in the doorway and nodded to her daughter. Penny turned and walked to Jon. He gathered her up in his arms.

"You've got the girl. Now the lady and I are going to walk to my car," Snake yelled. "I want everyone to back up behind the cars."

The officers moved back.

Lilly appeared first in the doorway, then Snake. He whispered something in her ear. She moved down the steps. Snake moved in tandem with her. Once they were standing on solid ground, he pulled her back against his body. They walked slowly to the van.

Jon whispered in Penny's ear, "When you hear the gunshot, drop to the ground and do not get up until I tell you it's okay." Her frightened gaze met his. "You understand?"

She nodded.

Jon prepared himself to explode into action.

As Lilly and Snake neared the van, Snake glanced around at the gathered law enforcement cars. He paused and commanded everyone to move back. His arm flexed around Lilly's neck, drawing her closer.

The cops complied.

They slowly moved toward the car readied for them. Stopping by the door, he whispered into Lilly's ear, "Open the door."

He released her so she could grab the door handle. When she bent down, a shot rang out. Blood sprayed out and Snake fell to the ground, dead.

Lilly screamed, covering her head.

Jon raced to her side. "Lilly, look at me."

Her frightened gaze locked with his. He couldn't tell if she'd been hurt. Blood and tissue covered her hair.

"Are you hurt?"

She stared at him, shaking.

He ran his hands up her back and into her hair. He could find no wounds. Pulling her into his arms with his lips against her forehead, he whispered, "You're okay, sweetheart."

"Mom," Penny yelled, coming out from behind one of the patrol cars. She froze, seeing her mother covered in blood.

Jon ripped his shirt off. "She's okay, Penny." He wrapped his shirt around Lilly's head.

Cruz Romero went to his car and pulled a blanket from the trunk. He offered it to Jon. He wrapped Lilly up and put her in his backseat. Penny joined her mother.

Ben Narvaiz stepped forward. "I'll call an ambulance."

Jon nodded and turned to Cruz. "Thank your officer for me. Tell him I'd like to meet him when I'm finished with the incident report."

Cruz held out his hand. "I'll tell Robert."

Jon turned to the car where Lilly and Penny sat. He'd been shaken to the core of his soul. When Snake dragged Lilly out of the trailer, he knew he couldn't have been the sniper because his feelings were involved in a big way. He would've traded his life for hers in a second.

No matter how hard he'd fought against it, he loved Lilly.

Now was he brave enough to act on those feelings? He didn't have an answer.

FOURTEEN

Lilly sat in clean clothes, her hair wild around her face. After she'd been checked over by the E.R. doctors, she'd been allowed to shower. Thankfully, she didn't remember too much of what ensued after she heard the gunshot. The important thing she remembered was Jon's voice asking her if she was okay. After she'd been released from the E.R. with clean clothes, the patrol officers had fed her and Penny and brought them to the police station.

She ran her fingers through Penny's hair, wondering where Jon was.

A female detective, Mai Rosales, came in and took Lilly and Penny to an interview room and questioned both of them. Penny told the detective how Snake had grabbed her, and how she'd woken up at the construction site. Penny noted that he'd been nice. When she'd asked to go home, he'd given her the soda and candy bar. She'd fallen asleep after that. When she woke, her mother was there.

Lilly gave her statement.

"Let me type these up and let you sign them," said Mai.

"Can we see Jon?" Lilly asked.

"Let me see if he's back from the scene yet."

When they were alone, Penny snuggled close to Lilly's side.

"Can I tell you something, Mom?"

Lilly pushed the hair away from Penny's face. "Of course."

"I was so scared when that man had me." She wrapped her arms around Lilly's waist.

"I was scared, too," Lilly confessed.

"What did they want?"

"Your dad had something they wanted."

"What was that guy going to do with it?"

Lilly closed her eyes. "I don't know." She wanted to assure her daughter that her father had intended to do the right thing, but she honestly didn't know what Peter had planned to do with the information.

Mai reappeared with two pieces of paper—the statements each of them had given. "Read them over. If they're right, please sign."

Lilly and Penny both quickly read the statements and signed. Mai gathered up the papers and left the room. Several minutes later, Dave appeared in the doorway.

"I'm here to drive you ladies home."

"What about Jon?" Penny asked.

Lilly's thoughts echoed her daughter's.

"He's tied up questioning Adam Finley."

"Who?" Lilly asked.

"The other guy who was at the trailer. He was your husband's old boss. It might take several more hours of talking to him. Jon is worried that maybe you would like to go home."

It could be hours before they saw Jon. Lilly realized she needed to get her daughter home. "Okay, Dave. Take us home."

Dave guided them by Jon's desk. "You might want your purse."

Lilly grabbed it.

Dave smiled. "Your cell phone is in your purse. That was quick thinking on your part."

"That was simply fear, Dave."

He leaned over and said, "Don't diminish what you did, Lilly. Without your cell phone, we never would've known where you were. Bravery is about acting in spite of our fear."

Lilly nodded. She didn't feel brave. She felt nervous and alone.

It was close to dinnertime when they arrived home. Dave walked them to the door. "The D.A. will probably be contacting you in the next few weeks."

"I understand," Lilly answered.

Dave walked back to the car and waved goodbye to them.

Once inside, Lilly went to the phone and called her parents in Florida, telling them what had happened. They offered to fly back home, but Lilly knew her father wasn't up to the trip. She convinced them not to come.

She waited for Jon to call. By one in the morning, she gave up.

Two weeks passed. Two long weeks of waiting for Jon to call. Penny had moped, wondering why Jon hadn't come to see them or called them. Even the beginning of the school year hadn't cheered Penny up.

Well, Lilly had had enough. She'd confront him head-on. Apparently, he could talk a good game, but couldn't deliver. When she arrived at the police station, she asked for David Sandoval. When he appeared in the lobby, Lilly asked him if Jon was there.

He smiled. "He's here. Want to talk to him?"

"I'm going to do more than talk," she reassured him.

Dave grinned. "Good."

His reaction threw Lilly.

"Come with me." He led her into the squad room. "Jon, someone's here to see you."

When Jon looked up, Lilly saw the haggard lines creasing his face.

"Go for it," Dave whispered in her ear.

She walked up to Jon's desk. "I have a bone to pick with you, mister. You might not have wanted to see me again, but I think you owe Penny an explanation. She asks about you all the time and misses you. She wonders what she did wrong to make you go away." She paused as she choked back tears. "I wonder the same thing myself."

Jon stood.

"Jon," she whispered, "I love you."

He remained frozen, staring at her.

She'd worried that maybe he held back because he didn't think she loved him. Or maybe he didn't want to gamble again with his heart.

"I understand if you don't want to risk your heart again. I'll pray God will heal you so that you can love again." She turned to race out of the room.

Suddenly she was in Jon's arms and his lips were on hers. And nothing mattered.

He broke off the kiss and his hands cupped her face. "Lilly, I love you. I was afraid to love again. The pain was so terrible when I lost my girls and wife. But the pain from not being with you and Penny, seeing your faces every day, is worse. I've been a coward. Please forgive me. I didn't realize how much courage it would take to open my heart again. I thought I'd never have another family and suddenly you and Penny dropped into my life."

She understood the risk he was taking. "I've thought of you every moment for the last two weeks."

He rested his forehead against hers. "Lilly, one thing that terrifies me is having another child die the way my girls did. I can't do that to another child."

If that had held him back, she understood his fear. "I understand, Jon. I never thought I'd love again, either. Then our paths crossed and my heart came to life no matter what my head said. I love you, and I have Penny. That's more than enough."

The expression in his eyes brightened, and his lips

slowly curved into a smile. "Let's go find Penny, then see Pastor Kent about a wedding."

She nodded and they walked out of the police station.

Dave yanked the phone off its cradle and called Marta with the good news.

EPILOGUE

Lilly sat in the church's fellowship hall. They'd finished the deliveries of vegetables from the garden. This harvest was the biggest they'd had, nearly four times larger than last year's and ten times the amount of that first harvest. After such a grand success, people had wanted to come back to the church to celebrate. It had been impromptu. People had brought food they'd made at home to share with each other. Zoe, who hated yard work with a passion, had even volunteered to help. She worked alongside Allison and Nancy. Nancy had convinced all of her fourth grade class to come and join in the harvesting.

Lilly glanced over at her husband. On his knee he bounced his six-month-old son, Tate. Lilly didn't carry the gene that had killed Jon's daughters, and Tate had been tested for the disease. He would grow up strong and whole. Penny, now ten, adored her little brother.

Penny had helped Connie and Caren plant their backyard garden. The three girls were the best of friends and got together frequently.

Jon raised his head and his gaze locked with Lilly's. In the depths of his eyes, she saw peace. And joy.

He'd been a full-time father to Penny for nearly two years now. She'd blossomed under his attention. He'd also been more active in the support group for the disease that had killed his daughters.

"Your garden is a great success," Jon said, nodding to the people around them.

"I had no idea any of this was possible," Lilly said, "but then, I didn't see the whole picture."

"But we know who does," Jon whispered.

"Amen," said Lilly. In her heart she added, *Thank You, Lord. Your gifts are beyond anything we can know.*

* * * * *

Dear Reader,

Jonathan Littedeer is a man close to my heart. After suffering through the deaths of his daughters and his wife, he tried to drink himself into oblivion. It was the faith of a young child who told him that Jesus could heal him that offered him hope. Sometimes the answers to our most trying questions are the simplest. Listen and be open to the hope God gives us. As I wrote Jon's story, I walked through his pain. Many times I found myself writing things and sitting back and saying "Wow." The scene in which Jon and Lilly discuss the picture of his wife and daughters on the mantel in his house is one such instance.

I hope you enjoy this journey from despair to triumph. As a child, I often visited family in New Mexico. There is something in that harsh landscape that calls to my soul, a beauty that touches me.

Enjoy.

Leann Harris

QUESTIONS FOR DISCUSSION

1. Lilly was conflicted by her newfound friendship with her ex-husband and her resentment of his behavior when they were married. Do you think her feelings were justified?

2. What do you think of the way Jon dealt with his grief? Have you ever let God comfort you in your grief?

3. Connie and Caren were quick to come to Uncle Jon's defense and Caren helped him find his way out of the darkness after the deaths of his wife and daughters. Have you experienced a situation where you heard the truth from an unusual source?

4. Lilly's job at the church included community outreach. Was the church garden a good idea? How can Christians reach out to the community around them?

5. How do we resolve the seeming contradiction between the Scriptures' claim that believing in Christ ensures salvation and James 2:14, which states, "What good is it, my brothers, if a man claims to have faith but has no deeds? Can such faith save him?"

6. Jon's feelings changed over the course of the story. He found his heart restored. Has that ever hap-

pened to you? How has God changed your heart so that you see joy and transcend sorrow? Or glimpse hope in the midst of darkness?

7. When Lilly initially showed up at the church, she didn't have any idea how God would use her. Has it ever happened to you that you started one thing, then found God using you to help others in a way you did not expect?

8. Lilly's friend Zoe was her advocate. Do you have a person in your life who helps you? Or have you been an advocate for another person?

9. Have you ever been in a situation where you were forced to make a choice between what was right and what was convenient, as Lilly's ex-husband was?

10. The book ends with Lilly and Jon having a new baby, who is healthy. Is this realistic? Have you ever had a miracle in your life?

11. Jon's partner, Dave, is a friend who saw Jon through the darkest time in his life. Have you ever had a friend like that? What did it mean to you?

12. Jon was afraid to love again. Were his feelings reasonable? Were they right? Beneficial?

When a young Roman woman is wrenched from the safety of her family and sold into slavery, she finds herself at the mercy of the most famous gladiator in Rome. In God's plan, a master and his slave just might fall in love….

Turn the page for a sneak preview of
THE GLADIATOR
by Carla Capshaw
Available in November 2009
from Love Inspired® Historical

Rome, 81 A.D.

Angry, unfamiliar voices penetrated Pelonia's awareness. Floating between wakefulness and dark, she couldn't budge. Every muscle ached. A sharp pain drummed against her skull.

The voices died away, then a woman's words broke through the haze.

"My name is Lucia. Can you hear me?" The woman pressed a cup of water to Pelonia's cracked lips. "What shall I call you?"

Pelonia coughed as the cool liquid trickled down her arid throat. "Pel...Pelonia."

"Do you remember what happened to you? You were struck on the head and injured. I've been giving you opium to soothe you, but you're far from recovered."

Her eyelids too heavy to open, Pelonia licked her chapped lips.

Gradually her mind began to make sense of her surroundings. The warmth must be sunshine, because the scent of wood smoke hung in the air. Her pallet was a coarse woolen blanket on the hard ground. Dirt clung to her skin and each of her sore muscles longed for the softness of her bed at home.

Home.

Where was she if not in the comfort of her father's Umbrian villa? Who was this woman Lucia? She couldn't remember.

Icy fingers of fear gripped her heart as one by one her memories returned. First the attack, then her father's murder. Raw grief squeezed her chest.

Confusion surrounded her. Where was her uncle? She remembered the slave caravan, his threat to sell her, but nothing more.

Panic forced her eyes open. She managed to focus on the young woman's face above her.

"The master will be here soon." A smile tilted Lucia's thin lips, but didn't touch her honey-brown eyes.

"Where…am I?" she asked, the words grating in her throat.

"You're in the home of Caros Viriathos."

The name meant nothing to Pelonia. She prayed God had delivered her into the hands of a kind man, someone who would help her contact her cousin Tiberia.

Her eyes closed with fatigue. "How…how long have I…been here?"

"Four days and this morning. You've been in and out of sleep. I'll order you a bowl of broth. You should eat to bolster your strength."

Four days, and she remembered nothing. Tiberia must be frantic wondering why she'd failed to attend her wedding.

She opened her eyes. "I must—"

"Don't speak. Now that you've woken, Gaius, our master's steward, says you have one week to recover. Then your labor begins."

"My cousin. I must…"

"You're a slave in the Ludus Maximus now. A possession of the *lanista,* Caros Viriathos."

Lanista? A vile *gladiator* trainer?

"No!"

Lucia crossed her arms over her buxom chest. "We will see."

Heavy footsteps crunched on the rushes strewn across the floor. The new arrival stopped out of Pelonia's view.

The nauseating ache in her head increased without mercy. What had she done to make God despise her?

Focusing on Lucia, she saw the young woman's face light with pleasure.

"Master," Lucia greeted, jumping to her feet. "The new slave is finally awake. She calls herself Pelonia. She's weak and the medicine I gave her has run its course."

"Then give her more if she needs it."

The man's deep voice poured over Pelonia like the soothing water of a bath. She turned her head, ignoring the jab of pain that pierced her skull.

"You mustn't move your head," Lucia snapped, "or you might injure yourself further."

Pelonia stiffened. She wasn't accustomed to taking orders from slaves.

Lucia glanced toward the door. "She's argumentative. I have a hunch she'll be difficult. She denies she's your slave."

Silence followed Lucia's remark. Would this man who claimed to own her kill or beat her? Was he a cruel barbarian?

She sensed him move closer. Her tension rose as if she were prey in the sights of a hungry lion. At last the lion crossed to where she could see him.

Sunlight streaming through the window enveloped the giant, giving his dark hair a golden glow. A crisp, light-colored tunic draped across his shoulders and chest contrasted sharply with the rich copper of his skin. Gold bands around his upper arms emphasized the thickness of his muscles, the physical power he held in check.

Her breath hitched in her throat. She could only stare. Without a doubt, the man could crush her if he chose.

"So, you are called Pelonia," he said. "And my healer believes you wish to fight me."

Her gaze locked with the unusual blue of his forceful glare. For the first time she understood how the Hebrew David must have suffered when he faced Goliath. Swallowing the lump of fear in her throat, she nodded. "If I must."

"If you must?" Caros eyed Pelonia with a mix of irritation and respect. With her tunic filthy and torn, her dark hair in disarray and her bruises healing, his new slave looked like a wounded goddess. But she was just an ordinary woman. Why did she think she could defy him?

"Then let the games begin," he said, his voice thick with mockery.

"You think…this…this is a game?" she asked faintly.

The roughness of her voice reminded him of her body's weakened condition—a frailty her spirit clearly didn't share. Crouching beside her, he ran his forefinger over the yellowed bruise on her cheek. She closed her eyes and sighed as though his touch somehow soothed her.

Her guileless response unnerved him. The need to protect her enveloped him, a sensation he hadn't known since the deaths of his mother and sisters. As a slave, he'd been beaten on many occasions in an effort to conquer his will. That no one ever succeeded was a matter of pride for him. Much to his surprise, he had no wish to see this girl broken, either.

"Of course it's a game. And I will be the victor."

Defiance flamed in the depths of her large, doe-brown eyes. She didn't speak and he admired her restraint when he could see she wanted to flay him.

"You might as well give in now, my prize. I own you whether you will it or not."

He gripped her chin and forced her to look at him.

"Admit it," he said. "Then you can return to your sleep."

She shook her head. "No. No one owns me…no one but my God."

"And who might your god be? Jupiter? Apollo? Or maybe you worship the god of the sea. Do you think Neptune will rescue you?"

"The Christ."

Caros wondered if she were a fool or had a wish for death. "Say that to the wrong person, Pelonia, and you'll find yourself facing the lions."

"I already am."

He laughed. "So you think of me as a ferocious beast?"

Her silence amused him all the more. "Good. It suits me well to know you realize I'm untamed and capable of tearing you limb from limb."

"Then do your worst. Death is better…than being owned."

Caros suddenly noticed Pelonia had grown pale and weaker still.

He berated himself for depleting her meager strength when he should have been encouraging her to heal. He lifted her into his arms.

She weighed no more than a laurel leaf. Had he pushed her to the brink of death?

Holding her tight against his chest, he whispered near her ear. "Tell me, *mea carissima*. What can I do to aid you? What can I do to ease your plight?"

"Find…Tiberia," she whispered, the dregs of her strength draining away. "And free me."

* * * * *

Will Pelonia ever convince Caros of who she is and where she truly belongs? Or will their growing love bind her to him for all time?

Find out in
THE GLADIATOR
by Carla Capshaw
Available in November 2009
from Love Inspired® Historical